"An extraordinary writer....The title story, 'Levitation,' is a master-piece." —JOHN LEONARD, *New York Times*

"She is a national treasure....There can no longer be any doubt that she is one of the finest writers of short fiction in America—or, indeed, anywhere." —SUSAN FROMBERG SCHAEFFER, *Chicago Tribune*

"She is one of the best!...Her stories shimmer with intelligence, they glory in language....She writes magically about magical events." —*Saturday Review*

"One of our finest living writers." —*Dallas Morning News*

"In Ozick's fiction, levitation is one miracle among many." —*Village Voice*

Obelisk

L E V I T A T I O N

Also by Cynthia Ozick

Bloodshed and Three Novellas
The Pagan Rabbi and Other Stories
Trust

Levitation

FIVE FICTIONS

Cynthia Ozick

A Dutton **Obelisk** Paperback

E.P. DUTTON, INC. / NEW YORK

Mama, Shiphra, O my maminke

תַּרְהִבֵנִי בְנַפְשִׁי עֹז

אָשִׂחֶה בְכָל־לַיְלָה מִטָּתִי,
בְּדִמְעָתִי עַרְשִׂי אַמְסֶה

Contents

L E V I T A T I O N

Levitation

A pair of novelists, husband and wife, gave a party. The husband was also an editor; he made his living at it. But really he was a novelist. His manner was powerless; he did not seem like an editor at all. He had a nice plain pale face, likable. His name was Feingold.

For love, and also because he had always known he did not want a Jewish wife, he married a minister's daughter. Lucy too had hoped to marry out of her tradition. (These words were hers. "Out of my tradition," she said. The idea fevered him.) At the age of twelve she felt herself to belong to the people of the Bible. ("A Hebrew," she said. His heart lurched, joy rocked him.) One night from the pulpit her father read a Psalm; all at once she saw how the Psalmist meant *her*; then and there she became an Ancient Hebrew.

She had huge, intent, sliding eyes, disconcertingly luminous, and copper hair, and a grave and timid way of saying honest things.

They were shy people, and rarely gave parties.

Each had published one novel. Hers was about domestic life; he wrote about Jews.

All the roil about the State of the Novel had passed them by. In the evening after the children had been put to bed, while the portable dishwasher rattled out its smell of burning motor oil, they sat down, she at her desk, he at his, and began to write. They wrote not without puzzlements and travail; nevertheless as naturally as birds. They were devoted to accuracy, psychological realism, and earnest truthfulness; also to virtue, and even to wit. Neither one was troubled by what had happened to the novel: all those declarations about the end of Character and Story. They were serene. Sometimes, closing up their notebooks for the night, it seemed to them that they were literary friends and lovers, like George Eliot and George Henry Lewes.

In bed they would revel in quantity and murmur distrustingly of theory. "Seven pages so far this week." "Nine-and-a-half, but I had to throw out four. A wrong tack." "Because you're doing first person. First person strangles. You can't get out of their skin." And so on. The one principle they agreed on was the importance of never writing about writers. Your protagonist always has to be someone *real*, with real work-in-the-world—a bureaucrat, a banker, an architect (ah, they envied Conrad his shipmasters!)—otherwise you fall into solipsism, narcissism, tedium, lack of appeal-to-the-common-reader; who knew what other perils.

This difficulty—seizing on a concrete subject—was mainly Lucy's. Feingold's novel—the one he was writing now—was about Menachem ben Zerach, survivor of a massacre of Jews in the town of Estella in Spain in 1328. From morning to midnight he hid under a pile of corpses, until a "compassionate knight" (this was the language of the history Feingold relied on) plucked him out and took him home to tend his wounds. Menachem was then twenty; his father and mother and four younger brothers had been cut down in the terror. Six thousand Jews died in a single day in March. Feingold wrote well about how the mild winds carried the salty fragrance of fresh blood, together with the ashes of Jewish houses, into the faces of the marauders. It was nevertheless a triumphant story: at the end Menachem ben Zerach becomes a renowned scholar.

"If you're going to tell about how after he gets to be a scholar he just sits there and *writes*," Lucy protested, "then you're doing the Forbidden Thing." But Feingold said he meant to concentrate on the massacre, and especially on the life of the "compassionate knight." What had brought him to this compassion? What sort of education? What did he read? Feingold would invent a journal for the compassionate knight, and quote from it. Into this journal the compassionate knight would direct all his gifts, passions, and private opinions.

"Solipsism," Lucy said. "Your compassionate knight is only another writer. Narcissism. Tedium."

They talked often about the Forbidden Thing. After a while they began to call it the Forbidden City, because not only were they (but Lucy especially) tempted to write—solipsistically, narcissistically, tediously, and without common appeal —about writers, but, more narrowly yet, about writers in New York.

"The compassionate knight," Lucy said, "lived on the Upper West Side of Estella. He lived on the Riverside Drive, the West End Avenue, of Estella. He lived in Estella on Central Park West."

The Feingolds lived on Central Park West.

In her novel—the published one, not the one she was writing now—Lucy had described, in the first person, where they lived:

> By now I have seen quite a few of those West Side apartments. They have mysterious layouts. Rooms with doors that go nowhere—turn the knob, open: a wall. Someone is snoring behind it, in another apartment. They have made two and three or even four and five flats out of these palaces. The toilet bowls have antique cracks that shimmer with moisture like old green rivers. Fluted columns and fireplaces. Artur Rubinstein once paid rent here. On a gilt piano he raced a sonata by Beethoven. The sounds went spinning like mercury. Breathings all lettered now. Editors. Critics. Books, old, old books, heavy as centuries. Shelves built into the cold fireplace; Freud on the grate, Marx on the hearth, Melville, Hawthorne, Emerson. Oh God, the weight, the weight.

Lucy felt herself to be a stylist; Feingold did not. He believed in putting one sentence after another. In his publishing house he had no influence. He was nervous about his decisions. He rejected most manuscripts because he was afraid of mistakes; every mistake lost money. It was a small house panting after profits; Feingold told Lucy that the only books his firm respected belonged to the accountants. Now and then he tried to smuggle in a novel after his own taste, and then he would be brutal to the writer. He knocked the paragraphs about until they were as sparse as his own. "God knows what you would do to mine," Lucy said; "bald man, bald prose." The horizon of Feingold's head shone. She never showed him her work. But they understood they were lucky in each other. They pitied every writer who was not married to a writer. Lucy said: "At least we have the same premises."

Volumes of Jewish history ran up and down their walls;

they belonged to Feingold. Lucy read only one book—it was
Emma—over and over again. Feingold did not have a "philosophical" mind. What he liked was event. Lucy liked to specu-
late and ruminate. She was slightly more intelligent than
Feingold. To strangers he seemed very mild. Lucy, when silent, was a tall copper statue.

They were both devoted to omniscience, but they were not
acute enough to see what they meant by it. They thought of
themselves as children with a puppet theater: they could make
anything at all happen, speak all the lines, with gloved hands
bring all the characters to shudders or leaps. They fancied
themselves in love with what they called "imagination." It was
not true. What they were addicted to was counterfeit pity, and
this was because they were absorbed by power, and were powerless.

They lived on pity, and therefore on gossip: who had been
childless for ten years, who had lost three successive jobs, who
was in danger of being fired, which agent's prestige had fallen,
who could not get his second novel published, who was *per-
sona non grata* at this or that magazine, who was drinking
seriously, who was a likely suicide, who was dreaming of divorce, who was secretly or flamboyantly sleeping with whom,
who was being snubbed, who counted or did not count; and
toward everyone in the least way victimized they appeared to
feel the most immoderate tenderness. They were, besides, extremely "psychological": kind listeners, helpful, lifting hot
palms they would gladly put to anyone's anguished temples.
They were attracted to bitter lives.

About their own lives they had a joke: they were "secondary-level" people. Feingold had a secondary-level job with
a secondary-level house. Lucy's own publisher was secondary-
level; even the address was Second Avenue. The reviews of
their books had been written by secondary-level reviewers. All
their friends were secondary-level: not the presidents or part-

ners of the respected firms, but copy editors and production assistants; not the glittering eagles of the intellectual organs, but the wearisome hacks of small Jewish journals; not the fiercely cold-hearted literary critics, but those wan and chattering daily reviewers of film. If they knew a playwright, he was off-off-Broadway in ambition and had not yet been produced. If they knew a painter, he lived in a loft and had exhibited only once, against the wire fence in the outdoor show at Washington Square in the spring. And this struck them as mean and unfair; they liked their friends, but other people—why not they?—were drawn into the deeper caverns of New York, among the lions.

New York! They risked their necks if they ventured out to Broadway for a loaf of bread after dark; muggers hid behind the seesaws in the playgrounds, junkies with knives hung upside down in the jungle gym. Every apartment a lit fortress; you admired the lamps and the locks, the triple locks on the caged-in windows, the double locks and the police rods on the doors, the lamps with timers set to make burglars think you were always at home. Footsteps in the corridor, the elevator's midnight grind; caution's muffled gasps. Their parents lived in Cleveland and St. Paul, and hardly ever dared to visit. All of this: grit and unsuitability (they might have owned a snowy lawn somewhere else); and no one said their names, no one had any curiosity about them, no one ever asked whether they were working on anything new. After half a year their books were remaindered for eighty-nine cents each. Anonymous mediocrities. They could not call themselves forgotten because they had never been noticed.

Lucy had a diagnosis: they were, both of them, sunk in a ghetto. Feingold persisted in his morbid investigations into Inquisitional autos-da-fé in this and that Iberian marketplace. She herself had supposed the inner life of a housebound woman—she cited *Emma*—to contain as much comedy as the cosmos. Jews and women! They were both beside the point. It was necessary to put aside pity; to look to the center; to abandon selflessness; to study power.

They drew up a list of luminaries. They invited Irving Howe, Susan Sontag, Alfred Kazin, and Leslie Fiedler. They invited Norman Podhoretz and Elizabeth Hardwick. They invited Philip Roth and Joyce Carol Oates and Norman Mailer and William Styron and Donald Barthelme and Jerzy Kosinski and Truman Capote. None of these came; all of them had unlisted numbers, or else machines that answered the telephone, or else were in Prague or Paris or out of town. Nevertheless the apartment filled up. It was a Saturday night in a chill November. Taxis whirled on patches of sleet. On the inside of the apartment door a mound of rainboots grew taller and taller. Two closets were packed tight with raincoats and fur coats; a heap of coats smelling of skunk and lamb fell tangled off a bed.

The party washed and turned like a sluggish tub; it lapped at all the walls of all the rooms. Lucy wore a long skirt, violet-colored, Feingold a lemon shirt and no tie. He looked paler than ever. The apartment had a wide center hall, itself the breadth of a room; the dining room opened off it to the left, the living room to the right. The three party-rooms shone like a triptych: it was as if you could fold them up and enclose everyone into darkness. The guests were free-standing figures in the niches of a cathedral; or else dressed-up cardboard dolls, with their drinks, and their costumes all meticulously hung with sashes and draped collars and little capes, the women's hair variously bound, the men's sprouting and spilling: fashion stalked, Feingold moped. He took in how it all flashed, manhattans and martinis, earrings and shoe-tips—he marveled, but knew it was a falsehood, even a figment. The great world was somewhere else. The conversation could fool you: how these people talked! From the conversation itself—grains of it, carried off, swallowed by new eddyings, swirl devouring swirl, every moment a permutation in the tableau of those free-standing figures or dolls, all of them afloat in a tub—from this or that hint or syllable you could imagine the whole universe in the process of ultimate comprehension. Human nature, the stars, history—the voices drummed and strummed. Lucy swam by blank-eyed, pushing a platter of mottled cheeses. Feingold seized her: "It's a waste!" She gazed back. He said, "No one's here!" Mournfully she rocked a stump of cheese; then he lost her.

He went into the living room: it was mainly empty, a few lumps on the sofa. The lumps wore business suits. The dining room was better. Something in formation: something around the big table: coffee cups shimmering to the brim, cake cut onto plates (the mock-Victorian rosebud plates from Boots's drug store in London: the year before their first boy was born Lucy and Feingold saw the Brontës' moors; Coleridge's house in Highgate; Lamb House, Rye, where Edith Wharton had tea with Henry James; Bloomsbury; the Cambridge stairs Forster had lived at the top of)—it seemed about to become a regular visit, with points of view, opinions; a discussion. The voices began to stumble; Feingold liked that, it was nearly human. But then, serving round the forks and paper napkins, he noticed the awful vivacity of their falsetto phrases: actors, theater chatter, who was directing whom, what was opening where; he hated actors. Shrill puppets. Brainless. A double row of faces around the table; gurgles of fools.

The center hall—swept clean. No one there but Lucy, lingering.

"Theater in the dining room," he said. "Junk."

"Film. I heard film."

"Film too," he conceded. "Junk. It's mobbed in there."

"Because they've got the cake. They've got all the food. The living room's got nothing."

"My God," he said, like a man choking, "do you realize *no one came?*"

The living room had—had once had—potato chips. The chips were gone, the carrot sticks eaten, of the celery sticks nothing left but threads. One olive in a dish; Feingold chopped it in two with vicious teeth. The business suits had disappeared. "It's awfully early," Lucy said; "a lot of people had to leave." "It's a cocktail party, that's what happens," Feingold said. "It isn't *exactly* a cocktail party," Lucy said. They sat down on the carpet in front of the fireless grate. "Is that a real fireplace?" someone inquired. "We never light it," Lucy said. "Do you light those candlesticks ever?" "They belonged to Jimmy's grandmother," Lucy said, "we never light them."

She crossed no-man's-land to the dining room. They were serious in there now. The subject was Chaplin's gestures.

In the living room Feingold despaired; no one asked him, he began to tell about the compassionate knight. A problem of ego, he said: compassion being superconsciousness of one's own pride. Not that he believed this; he only thought it provocative to say something original, even if a little muddled. But no one responded. Feingold looked up. "Can't you light that fire?" said a man. "All right," Feingold said. He rolled a paper log made of last Sunday's *Times* and laid a match on it. A flame as clear as a streetlight whitened the faces of the sofa-sitters. He recognized a friend of his from the Seminary—he had what Lucy called "theological" friends—and then and there, really very suddenly, Feingold wanted to talk about God. Or, if not God, then certain historical atrocities, abominations: to wit, the crime of the French nobleman Draconet, a proud Crusader, who in the spring of the year 1247 arrested all the Jews of the province of Vienne, castrated the men, and tore off the breasts of the women; some he did not mutilate, and only cut in two. It interested Feingold that Magna Carta and the Jewish badge of shame were issued in the same year, and that less than a century afterward all the Jews were driven out of England, even families who had been settled there seven or eight generations. He had a soft spot for Pope Clement IV, who absolved the Jews from responsibility for the Black Death. "The plague takes the Jews themselves," the Pope said. Feingold knew innumerable stories about forced conversions, he felt at home with these thoughts, comfortable, the chairs seemed dense with family. He wondered whether it would be appropriate—at a cocktail party, after all!—to inquire after the status of the Seminary friend's agnosticism: was it merely that God had stepped out of history, left the room for a moment, so to speak, without a pass, or was there no Creator to begin with, nothing had been created, the world was a chimera, a solipsist's delusion?

Lucy was uneasy with the friend from the Seminary; he was the one who had administered her conversion, and every encounter was like a new stage in a perpetual examination. She was glad there was no Jewish catechism. Was she a backslider? Anyhow she felt tested. Sometimes she spoke of Jesus to the children. She looked around—her great eyes wheeled—and saw that everyone in the living room was a Jew.

There were Jews in the dining room too, but the unruffled, devil-may-care kind: the humorists, the painters, film reviewers who went off to studio showings of *Screw on Screen* on the eve of the Day of Atonement. Mostly there were Gentiles in the dining room. Nearly the whole cake was gone. She took the last piece, cubed it on a paper plate, and carried it back to the living room. She blamed Feingold, he was having one of his spasms of fanaticism. Everyone normal, everyone with sense—the humanists and humorists, for instance—would want to keep away. What was he now, after all, but one of those boring autodidacts who spew out everything they read? He was doing it for spite, because no one had come. There he was, telling about the blood-libel. Little Hugh of Lincoln.

How in London, in 1279, Jews were torn to pieces by horses, on a charge of having crucified a Christian child. How in 1285, in Munich, a mob burned down a synagogue on the same pretext. At Eastertime in Mainz two years earlier. Three centuries of beatified child martyrs, some of them figments, all called "Little Saints." The Holy Niño of LaGuardia. Feingold was crazed by these tales, he drank them like a vampire. Lucy stuck a square of chocolate cake in his mouth to shut him up. Feingold was waiting for a voice. The friend from the Seminary, pragmatic, licked off his bit of cake hungrily. It was a cake sent from home, packed by his wife in a plastic bag, to make sure there was something to eat. It was a guaranteed no-lard cake. They were all ravenous. The fire crumpled out in big paper cinders.

The friend from the Seminary had brought a friend. Lucy examined him: she knew how to give catechisms of her own, she was not a novelist for nothing. She catechized and catalogued: a refugee. Fingers like long wax candles, snuffed at the nails. Black sockets: was he blind? It was hard to tell where the eyes were under that ledge of skull. Skull for a head, but such a cushioned mouth, such lips, such orderly expressive teeth. Such a bone in such a dry wrist. A nose like a saint's. The face of Jesus. He whispered. Everyone leaned over to hear. He was Feingold's voice: the voice Feingold was waiting for.

"Come to modern times," the voice urged. "Come to yesterday." Lucy was right: she could tell a refugee in an instant, even before she heard any accent. They all reminded her of her father. She put away this insight (the resemblance of Presbyterian ministers to Hitler refugees) to talk over with Feingold later: it was nicely analytical, it had enough mystery to satisfy. "Yesterday," the refugee said, "the eyes of God were shut." And Lucy saw him shut his hidden eyes in their tunnels. "Shut," he said, "like iron doors"—a voice of such nobility that Lucy thought immediately of that eerie passage in Genesis where the voice of the Lord God walks in the Garden in the cool of the day and calls to Adam, "Where are you?"

They all listened with a terrible intensity. Again Lucy looked around. It pained her how intense Jews could be, though she too was intense. But she was intense because her brain was roiling with ardor, she wooed mind-pictures, she was a novelist. *They* were intense all the time; she supposed the grocers among them were as intense as any novelist; was it because they had been Chosen, was it because they pitied themselves every breathing moment?

Pity and shock stood in all their faces.

The refugee was telling a story. "I witnessed it," he said, "I am the witness." Horror; sadism; corpses. As if—Lucy took the image from the elusive wind that was his voice in its whisper—as if hundreds and hundreds of Crucifixions were all happening at once. She visualized a hillside with multitudes of crosses, and bodies dropping down from big bloody nails. Every Jew was Jesus. That was the only way Lucy could get hold of it: otherwise it was only a movie. She had seen all the movies, the truth was she could feel nothing. That same bulldozer shoveling those same sticks of skeletons, that same little boy in a cap with twisted mouth and his hands in the air—if there had been a camera at the Crucifixion Christianity would collapse, no one would ever feel anything about it. Cruelty came out of the imagination, and had to be witnessed by the imagination.

All the same, she listened. What he told was exactly like the movies. A gray scene, a scrubby hill, a ravine. Germans in helmets, with shining tar-black belts, wearing gloves. A ragged bundle of Jews at the lip of the ravine—an old grandmother, a child or two, a couple in their forties. All the faces stained with grayness, the stubble on the ground stained gray, the clothes on them limp as shrouds but immobile, as if they were already under the dirt, shut off from breezes, as if they were already stone. The refugee's whisper carved them like sculptures—there they stood, a shadowy stone asterisk of Jews, you could see their nostrils, open as skulls, the stony round ears of the children, the grandmother's awful twig of a neck, the father and mother grasping the children but strangers to each other, not a touch between them, the grandmother cast out, claiming no one and not claimed, all prayerless stone gums. There they stood. For a long while the refugee's voice pinched them and held them, so that you had to look. His voice made Lucy look and look. He pierced the figures through with his whisper. Then he let the shots come. The figures never teetered, never shook: the stoniness broke all at once and they fell cleanly, like sacks, into the ravine. Immediately they were in a heap, with random limbs all tangled together. The refugee's voice like a camera brought a German boot to the edge of the ravine. The boot kicked sand. It kicked and kicked, the sand poured over the family of sacks.

Then Lucy saw the fingers of the listeners—all their fingers were stretched out.

The room began to lift. It ascended. It rose like an ark on waters. Lucy said inside her mind, "This chamber of Jews." It seemed to her that the room was levitating on the little grains of the refugee's whisper. She felt herself alone at the bottom, below the floorboards, while the room floated upward, carrying Jews. Why did it not take her too? Only Jesus could take her. They were being kidnapped, these Jews, by a messenger from the land of the dead. The man had a power. Already he was in the shadow of another tale: she promised herself she would not listen, only Jesus could make her listen. The room was ascending. Above her head it grew smaller and smaller, more and more remote, it fled deeper and deeper into upwardness.

She craned after it. Wouldn't it bump into the apartment

upstairs? It was like watching the underside of an elevator, all dirty and hairy, with dust-roots wagging. The black floor moved higher and higher. It was getting free of her, into loftiness, lifting Jews.

The glory of their martyrdom.

Under the rising eave Lucy had an illumination: she saw herself with the children in a little city park. A Sunday afternoon early in May. Feingold has stayed home to nap, and Lucy and the children find seats on a bench and wait for the unusual music to begin. The room is still levitating, but inside Lucy's illumination the boys are chasing birds. They run away from Lucy, they return, they leave. They surround a pigeon. They do not touch the pigeon; Lucy has forbidden it. She has read that city pigeons carry meningitis. A little boy in Red Bank, New Jersey, contracted sleeping sickness from touching a pigeon; after six years, he is still asleep. In his sleep he has grown from a child to an adolescent; puberty has come on him in his sleep, his testicles have dropped down, a benign blond beard glints mildly on his cheeks. His parents weep and weep. He is still asleep. No instruments or players are visible. A woman steps out onto a platform. She is an anthropologist from the Smithsonian Institution in Washington, D.C. She explains that there will be no "entertainment" in the usual sense; there will be no "entertainers." The players will not be artists; they will be "real peasants." They have been brought over from Messina, from Calabria. They are shepherds, goatherds. They will sing and dance and play just as they do when they come down from the hills to while away the evenings in the taverns. They will play the instruments that scare away the wolves from the flock. They will sing the songs that celebrate the Madonna of Love. A dozen men file onto the platform. They have heavy faces that do not smile. They have heavy dark skins, cratered and leathery. They have ears and noses that look like dried twisted clay. They have gold teeth. They have no teeth. Some are young; most are in their middle years. One is very old, he wears bells on his fingers. One has an instrument like a butter churn: he shoves a stick in and out of a hole in a wooden tub held under his arm, and a rattling screech spurts out of it. One blows on two slender pipes simultaneously. One has a long strap, which he rubs. One has a frame of bicycle bells; a descendant of the bells the priests used to beat in the temple of Minerva.

The anthropologist is still explaining everything. She explains the "male" instrument: three wooden knockers; the innermost one lunges up and down between the other two. The songs, she explains, are mainly erotic. The dances are suggestive.

The unusual music commences. The park has filled with Italians—greenhorns from Sicily, settled New Yorkers from Naples. An ancient people. They clap. The old man with the bells on his fingers points his dusty shoe-toes and slowly follows a circle of his own. His eyes are in trance, he squats, he ascends. The anthropologist explains that up-and-down dancing can also be found in parts of Africa. The singers wail like Arabs; the anthropologist notes that the Arab conquest covered the southernmost portion of the Italian boot for two hundred years. The whole chorus of peasants sings in a dialect of archaic Greek; the language has survived in the old songs, the anthropologist explains. The crowd is laughing and stamping. They click their fingers and sway. Lucy's boys are bored. They watch the man with the finger-bells; they watch the wooden male pump up and down. Everyone is clapping, stamping, clicking, swaying, thumping. The wailing goes on and on, faster and faster. The singers are dancers, the dancers are singers, they turn and turn, they are smiling the drugged smiles of dervishes. At home they grow flowers. They follow the sheep into the deep grass. They drink wine in the taverns at night. Calabria and Sicily in New York, sans wives, in sweat-blotched shirts and wrinkled dusty pants, gasping before strangers who have never smelled the sweetness of their village grasses!

Now the anthropologist from the Smithsonian has vanished out of Lucy's illumination. A pair of dancers seize each other. Leg winds over leg, belly into belly, each man hopping on a single free leg. Intertwined, they squat and rise, squat and rise. Old Hellenic syllables fly from them. They send out high elastic cries. They celebrate the Madonna, giver of fertility and fecundity. Lucy is glorified. She is exalted. She comprehends. Not that the musicians are peasants, not that their faces and feet and necks and wrists are blown grass and red earth. An enlightenment comes on her: she sees what is eternal: before the Madonna there was Venus; before Venus, Aphrodite; before Aphrodite, Astarte. The womb of the goddess is garden, lamb, and babe. She is the river and the waterfall. She causes grave men of business—goatherds are men of business—to cavort and to flash their gold teeth. She induces them to blow, beat, rub, shake and scrape objects so that music will drop out of them.

Inside Lucy's illumination the dancers are seething. They are writhing. For the sake of the goddess, for the sake of the womb of the goddess, they are turning into serpents. When they grow still they are earth. They are from always to always. Nature is their pulse. Lucy sees: she understands: the gods are God. How terrible to have given up Jesus, a man like these, made of earth like these, with a pulse like these, God entering nature to become god! Jesus, no more miraculous than an ordinary goatherd; is a goatherd miracle? Is a leaf? A nut, a pit, a core, a seed, a stone? Everything is miracle! Lucy sees how she has abandoned nature, how she has lost true religion on account of the God of the Jews. The boys are on their bellies on the ground, digging it up with sticks. They dig and dig: little holes with mounds beside them. They fill them with peach pits, cherry pits, cantaloupe rinds. The Sicilians and Neapolitans pick up their baskets and purses and shopping bags and leave. The benches smell of eaten fruit, running juices, insect-mobbed. The stage is clean.

The living room has escaped altogether. It is very high and extremely small, no wider than the moon on Lucy's thumbnail. It is still sailing upward, and the voices of those on board are so faint that Lucy almost loses them. But she knows which word it is they mainly use. How long can they go on about it? How long? A morbid cud-chewing. Death and death and death. The word is less a human word than an animal's cry; a crow's. Caw caw. It belongs to storms, floods, avalanches. Acts of God. "Holocaust," someone caws dimly from above; she knows it must be Feingold. He always says this word over and over and over. History is bad for him: how little it makes him seem! Lucy decides it is possible to become jaded by atrocity. She is bored by the shootings and the gas and the camps, she is not ashamed to admit this. They are as tiresome as prayer. Repetition diminishes conviction; she is thinking of her father leading the same hymns week after week. If you said the same prayer over and over again, wouldn't your brain turn out to be no better than a prayer wheel?

In the dining room all the springs were running down. It was stale in there, a failed party. They were drinking beer or Coke or whiskey-and-water and playing with the cake crumbs on the tablecloth. There was still some cheese left on a plate, and half a bowl of salted peanuts. "The impact of Romantic Individualism," one of the humanists objected. "At the Frick?" "I never saw that." "They certainly are deliberate, you have to say that for them." Lucy, leaning abandoned against the door, tried to tune in. The relief of hearing atheists. A jacket designer who worked in Feingold's art department came in carrying a coat. Feingold had invited her because she was newly divorced; she was afraid to live alone. She was afraid of

ambushed in her basement while doing laundry.
here's Jimmy?" the jacket designer asked. "In the other
om." "Say goodbye for me, will you?" "Goodbye," Lucy
said. The humanists—Lucy saw how they were all compassionate knights—stood up. A puddle from an overturned
saucer was leaking onto the floor. "Oh, I'll get that," Lucy told
the knights, "don't think another thought about it."

Overhead Feingold and the refugee are riding the living
room. Their words are specks. All the Jews are in the air.

Puttermesser:
Her Work History,
Her Ancestry,
Her Afterlife

Puttermesser was thirty-four, a lawyer. She was also something of a feminist, not crazy, but she resented having "Miss" put in front of her name; she thought it pointedly discriminatory, she wanted to be a lawyer among lawyers. Though she was no virgin she lived alone, but idiosyncratically—in the Bronx, on the Grand Concourse, among other people's decaying old parents. Her own had moved to Miami Beach; in furry slippers left over from high school she roamed the same endlessly mazy apartment she had grown up in, her aging piano sheets still on top of the upright with the teacher's X marks on them showing where she should practice up to. Puttermesser always pushed a little ahead of the actual assignment; in school too. Her teachers told her mother she was "highly motivated," "achievement oriented." Also she had "scholastic drive." Her mother wrote all these things down in a notebook, kept it always, and took it with her to Florida in case she should die there. Puttermesser had a younger sister who was also highly motivated, but she had married an Indian, a Parsee chemist, and gone to live in Calcutta. Already the sister had four children and seven saris of various fabrics.

Puttermesser went on studying. In law school they called her a grind, a competitive-compulsive, an egomaniac out for aggrandizement. But ego was no part of it; she was looking to solve something, she did not know what. At the back of the linen closet she found a stack of her father's old shirt cardboards (her mother was provident, stingy: in kitchen drawers Puttermesser still discovered folded squares of used ancient waxed paper, million-creased into whiteness, cheese-smelling, nesting small unidentifiable wormlets); so behind the riser pipe in the bathroom Puttermesser kept weeks' worth of Sunday *Times* crossword puzzles stapled to these laundry boards and worked on them indiscriminately. She played chess against herself, and was always victor over the color she had decided to identify with. She organized tort cases on index cards. It was not that she intended to remember everything: situations—it was her tendency to call intellectual problems "situations"—slipped into her mind like butter into a bottle.

A letter came from her mother in Florida:

Dear Ruth,

I know you won't believe this but I swear it's true the other day Daddy was walking on the Avenue and who should he run into but Mrs. Zaretsky, the thin one from Burnside not the stout one from Davidson, you remember her Joel? Well he's divorced now no children thank God so he's free as a bird as they say his ex the poor thing couldn't conceive. *He* had tests he's O.K. He's only an accountant not good enough for you because God knows

I never forget the day you made Law Review but you should come down just to see what a tender type he grew into. Every tragedy has its good side Mrs. Zaretsky says he comes down now practically whenever she calls him long distance. Daddy said to Mrs. Zaretsky well, an accountant, you didn't overeducate your son anyhow, with daughters it's different. But don't take this to heart honey Daddy is as proud as I am of your achievements. Why don't you write we didn't hear from you too long busy is busy but parents are parents.

Puttermesser had a Jewish face and a modicum of American distrust of it. She resembled no poster she had ever seen: with a Negroid passion she hated the Breck shampoo girl, so blond and bland and pale-mouthed; she boycotted Breck because of the golden-haired posters, all crudely idealized, an American wet dream, in the subway. Puttermesser's hair came in bouncing scallops—layered waves from scalp to tip, like imbricated roofing tile. It was nearly black and had a way of sometimes sticking straight out. Her nose had thick, well-haired, uneven nostrils, the right one noticeably wider than the other. Her eyes were small, the lashes short, invisible. She had the median Mongol lid—one of those Jewish faces with a vaguely Oriental cast. With all this, it was a fact she was not bad-looking. She had a good skin with, so far, few lines or pits or signs of looseness-to-come. Her jaw was pleasing—a baby jowl appeared only when she put her head deep in a book.

In bed she studied Hebrew grammar. The permutations of the triple-lettered root elated her: how was it possible that a whole language, hence a whole literature, a civilization even, should rest on the pure presence of three letters of the alphabet? The Hebrew verb, a stunning mechanism: three letters, whichever fated three, could command all possibility simply by a change in their pronunciation, or the addition of a wing-letter fore and aft. Every conceivable utterance blossomed from this trinity. It seemed to her not so much a language for expression as a code for the world's design, indissoluble, pre-determined, translucent. The idea of the grammar of Hebrew turned Puttermesser's brain into a palace, a sort of Vatican; inside its corridors she walked from one resplendent triptych to another.

She wrote her mother a letter refusing to come to Florida to look over the divorced accountant's tenderness. She explained her life again; she explained it by indirection. She wrote:

> I have a cynical apperception of power, due no doubt to my current job. You probably haven't heard of the Office for Visas and Registration, OVIR for short. It's located on Ogaryova Street, in Moscow, U.S.S.R. I could enumer-ate for you a few of the innumerable bureaucratic atro-cities of OVIR, not that anyone knows them all. But I could give you a list of the names of all those criminals, down to the women clerks, Yefimova, Korolova, Akulova, Arkhipova, Izrailova, all of them on Kolpachni Street in an office headed by Zolotukhin, the assistant to Colonel Smyrnov, who's under Ovchinikov, who is second in com-mand to General Viryein, only Viryein and Ovchinikov aren't on Kolpachni Street, they're the ones in the head office—the M.D.V., Internal Affairs Ministry—on Oga-ryova Street. Some day all the Soviet Jews will come out of the spider's clutches of these people and be free. Please explain to Daddy that this is one of the highest priorities of my life at this time in my personal history. Do you think a Joel Zaretsky can share such a vision?

Immediately after law school, Puttermesser entered the firm of Midland, Reid & Cockleberry. It was a blueblood Wall Street firm, and Puttermesser, hired for her brains and ingratiating (read: immigrant-like) industry, was put into a back office to hunt up all-fours cases for the men up front. Though a Jew and a woman, she felt little discrimination: the back office was chiefly the repository of unmitigated drudgery and therefore of usable youth. Often enough it kept its lights burning till three in the morning. It was right that the Top Rung of law school should earn you the Bottom of the Ladder in the actual world of all-fours. The wonderful thing was the fact of the Ladder itself. And though she was the only woman, Puttermesser was not the only Jew. Three Jews a year joined the back precincts of Midland, Reid (four the year Puttermesser came, which meant they thought "woman" more than "Jew" at the sight of her). Three Jews a year left—not the same three. Lunchtime was difficult. Most of the young men went to one or two athletic clubs nearby to "work out"; Puttermesser ate from a paper bag at her desk, along with the other Jews, and this was strange: the young male Jews appeared to be as committed to the squash courts as the others. Alas, the athletic clubs would not have them, and this too was preternatural— the young Jews were indistinguishable from the others. They bought the same suits from the same tailors, wore precisely the same shirts and shoes, were careful to avoid tie clips and to be barbered a good deal shorter than the wild men of the streets, though a bit longer than the prigs in the banks.

Puttermesser remembered what Anatole France said of Dreyfus: that he was the same type as the officers who condemned him. "In their shoes he would have condemned himself."

Only their accents fell short of being identical: the "a" a shade too far into the nose, the "i" with its telltale elongation, had long ago spread from Brooklyn to Great Neck, from Puttermesser's Bronx to Scarsdale. These two influential vowels had the uncanny faculty of disqualifying them for promotion. The squash players, meanwhile, moved out of the back offices into the front offices. One or two of them were groomed—curried, fed sugar, led out by the muzzle—for partnership: were called out to lunch with thin and easeful clients, spent an afternoon in the dining room of one of the big sleek banks, and, in short, developed the creamy cheeks and bland habits of the always-comfortable.

The Jews, by contrast, grew more anxious, hissed together meanly among the urinals (Puttermesser, in the ladies' room next door, could hear malcontent rumblings in the connecting plumbing), became perfectionist and uncasual, quibbled bitterly, with stabbing forefingers, over principles, and all in all began to look and act less like superannuated college athletes and more like Jews. Then they left. They left of their own choice; no one shut them out.

Puttermesser left too, weary of so much chivalry—the partners in particular were excessively gracious to her, and treated her like a fellow-aristocrat. Puttermesser supposed this was because *she* did not say "a" in her nose or elongate her "i," and above all she did not dentalize her "t," "d," or "l," keeping them all back against the upper palate. Long ago her speech had been "standardized" by the drilling of fanatical teachers, elocutionary missionaries hired out of the Midwest by Puttermesser's prize high school, until almost all the regionalism was drained out; except for the pace of her syllables, which had a New York deliberateness, Puttermesser could have come from anywhere. She was every bit as American as her grandfather in his captain's hat. From Castle Garden to blue New England mists, her father's father, hat-and-neckwear peddler to Yankees! In Puttermesser's veins Providence, Rhode Island, beat richly. It seemed to her the partners felt this.

Then she remembered that Dreyfus spoke perfect French, and was the perfect Frenchman.

For farewell she was taken out to a public restaurant—the clubs the partners belonged to (they explained) did not allow women—and apologized to.

"We're sorry to lose you," one said, and the other said, "No one for you in this outfit for under the canvas, hah?"

"The canvas?" Puttermesser said.

"Wedding canopy," said the partner, with a wink. "Or do they make them out of sheepskin—I forget."

"An interesting custom. I hear you people break the dishes at a wedding too," said the second partner.

An anthropological meal. They explored the rites of her tribe. She had not known she was strange to them. Their beautiful manners were the cautiousness you adopt when you visit the interior: Dr. Livingstone, I presume? They shook hands and wished her luck, and at that moment, so close to their faces with those moist smile-ruts flowing from the sides of their waferlike noses punctured by narrow, even nostrils, Puttermesser was astonished into noticing how strange *they* were— so many luncheon martinis inside their bellies, and such beautiful manners even while drunk, and, important though they were, insignificant though she was, the fine ceremonial fact of their having brought her to this carpeted place. Their eyes were blue. Their necks were clean. How closely they were shaven!—like men who grew no hair at all. Yet hairs curled inside their ears. They let her take away all her memo pads with her name printed on them. She was impressed by their courtesy, their benevolence, through which they always got their way. She had given them three years of meticulous anonymous research, deep deep nights going after precedents, dates, lost issues, faded faint politics; for their sakes she had yielded up those howling morning headaches and half a diopter's worth of sight in both eyes. Brilliant students make good aides. They were pleased though not regretful. She was replaceable: a clever black had been hired only that morning.

The palace they led her to at the end of it all was theirs by divine right: in which they believed, on which they acted. They were benevolent because benevolence was theirs to dispense.

She went to work for the Department of Receipts and Disbursements. Her title was Assistant Corporation Counsel—it had no meaning, it was part of the subspeech on which bureaucracy relies. Of the many who held this title most were Italians and Jews, and again Puttermesser was the only woman. In this great City office there were no ceremonies and no manners: gross shouts, ignorant clerks, slovenliness, litter on the floors, grit stuck all over antiquated books. The ladies' room reeked: the women urinated standing up, and hot urine splashed on the toilet seats and onto the muddy tiles.

The successive heads of this department were called Commissioners. They were all political appointees—scavengers after spoils. Puttermesser herself was not quite a civil servant and not quite *not* a civil servant—one of those amphibious creatures hanging between base contempt and bare decency; but she soon felt the ignominy of belonging to that mean swarm of City employees rooted bleakly in cells inside the honeycomb of the Municipal Building. It was a monstrous place, gray everywhere, abundantly tunneled, with multitudes of corridors and stairs and shafts, a kind of swollen doom through which the bickering of small-voiced officials whinnied. At the same time there were always curious farm sounds —in the summer the steady cricket of the air-conditioning, in the winter the gnash and croak of old radiators. Nevertheless the windows were broad and high and stupendously filled with light; they looked out on the whole lower island of Manhattan, revealed *as* an island, down to the Battery, all crusted over with the dried lava of shape and shape: rectangle over square, and square over spire. At noon the dark gongs of St. Andrew's boomed their wild and stately strokes.

To Puttermesser all this meant she had come down in the world. Here she was not even a curiosity. No one noticed a Jew. Unlike the partners at Midland, Reid, the Commissioners did not travel out among their subjects and were rarely seen. Instead they were like shut-up kings in a tower, and suffered from rumors.

But Puttermesser discovered that in City life all rumors are true. Putative turncoats are genuine turncoats. All whispered knifings have happened: officials reputed to be about to topple, topple. So far Puttermesser had lasted through two elections, seeing the powerful become powerless and the formerly powerless inflate themselves overnight, like gigantic winds, to suck out the victory of the short run. When one Administration was razed, for the moment custom seemed leveled with it, everything that smelled of "before," of "the old way"—but only at first. The early fits of innovation subsided, and gradually the old way of doing things crept back, covering everything over, like grass, as if the building and its workers were together some inexorable vegetable organism with its own laws of subsistence. The civil servants were grass. Nothing destroyed them, they were stronger than the pavement, they were stronger than time. The Administration might turn on its hinge, throwing out one lot of patronage eaters and gathering in the new lot: the work went on. They might put in fresh carpeting in the new Deputy's office, or a private toilet in the new Commissioner's, and change the clerks' light bulbs to a lower wattage, and design an extravagant new colophon for a useless old document—they might do anything they liked: the work went on as before. The organism breathed, it comprehended itself.

So there was nothing for the Commissioner to do, and he knew it, and the organism knew it. For a very great salary the Commissioner shut his door and cleaned his nails behind it with one of the shining tools of a fancy Swiss knife, and had a secretary who was rude to everyone, and made dozens of tele-phone calls every day.

The current one was a rich and foolish playboy who had given the Mayor money for his campaign. All the high officials of every department were either men who had given the Mayor money or else courtiers who had humiliated themselves for him in the political clubhouse—mainly by flattering the clubhouse boss, who before any election was already a secret mayor and dictated the patronage lists. But the current Com-missioner owed nothing to the boss because he had given the Mayor money and was the Mayor's own appointee; and any-how he would have little to do with the boss because he had little to do with any Italian. The boss was a gentlemanly Neapolitan named Fiore, the chairman of the board of a bank; but still, he was only an Italian, and the Commissioner cared chiefly for blue-eyed bankers. He used his telephone to make luncheon appointments with them, and sometimes tennis. He himself was a blue-eyed Guggenheim, a German Jew, but not one of the grand philanthropic Guggenheims. The name was a cunning coincidence (cut down from Guggenheimer), and he was rich enough to be taken for one of the real Guggenheims, who thought him an upstart and disowned him. Grandeur de-mands discreetness; he was so discreetly disowned that no one knew it, not even the Rockefeller he had met at Choate.

This Commissioner was a handsome, timid man, still young, and good at boating; on weekends he wore sneakers and cultivated the friendship of the dynasties—Sulzbergers and Warburgs, who let him eat with them but warned their daughters against him. He had dropped out of two colleges and finally graduated from the third by getting a term-paper factory to plagiarize his reports. He was harmless and simple-minded, still devoted to his brainy late father, and frightened to death of news conferences. He understood nothing: art appreciation had been his best subject (he was attracted to

Renaissance nudes), economics his worst. If someone asked, "How much does the City invest every day?" or "Is there any Constitutional bar against revenue from commuters?" or "What is your opinion about taxing exempt properties?" his pulse would catch in his throat, making his nose run, and he had to say he was pressed for time and would let them have the answers from his Deputy in charge of the Treasury. Sometimes he would even call on Puttermesser for an answer.

Now if this were an optimistic portrait, exactly here is where Puttermesser's emotional life would begin to grind itself into evidence. Her biography would proceed romantically, the rich young Commissioner of the Department of Receipts and Disbursements would fall in love with her. She would convert him to intelligence and to the cause of Soviet Jewry. He would abandon boating and the pursuit of bluebloods. Puttermesser would end her work history abruptly and move on to a bower in a fine suburb.

This is not to be. Puttermesser will always be an employee in the Municipal Building. She will always behold Brooklyn Bridge through its windows; also sunsets of high glory, bringing her religious pangs. She will not marry. Perhaps she will undertake a long-term affair with Vogel, the Deputy in charge of the Treasury; perhaps not.

The difficulty with Puttermesser is that she is loyal to certain environments.

Puttermesser, while working in the Municipal Building, had a luxuriant dream, a dream of *gan eydn*—a term and notion handed on from her great-uncle Zindel, a former shammes in a shul that had been torn down. In this reconstituted Garden of Eden, which is to say in the World to Come, Puttermesser, who was not afflicted with quotidian uncertainty in the Present World, had even more certainty of her aims. With her weakness for fudge (others of her age, class, and character had advanced to martinis, at least to ginger ale; Puttermesser still drank ice cream with cola, despised mints as too tingly, eschewed salty liver canapés, hunted down chocolate babies, Kraft caramels, Mary Janes, Milky Ways, peanut brittle, and immediately afterward furiously brushed her teeth, scrubbing off guilt)—with all this nasty self-indulgence, she was nevertheless very thin and unironic. Or: to postulate an afterlife was her single irony—a game in the head not unlike a melting fudge cube held against the upper palate.

There, at any rate, Puttermesser would sit, in Eden, under a middle-sized tree, in the solid blaze of an infinite heart-of-summer July, green, green, green everywhere, green above and green below, herself gleaming and made glorious by sweat, every itch annihilated, fecundity dismissed. And there Puttermesser would, as she imagined it, *take in*. Ready to her left hand, the box of fudge (rather like the fudge sold to the lower school by the eighth-grade cooking class in P.S. 74, The Bronx, circa 1942); ready to her right hand, a borrowed steeple of library books: for into Eden the Crotona Park Branch has ascended intact, sans librarians and fines, but with its delectable terrestrial binding-glue fragrances unevaporated.

Here Puttermesser sits. Day after celestial day, perfection of desire upon perfection of contemplation, into the exaltations of an uninterrupted forever, she eats fudge in human shape (once known—no use covering this up—as nigger babies), or fudge in square shapes (and in Eden there is no tooth decay); and she reads. Puttermesser reads and reads. Her eyes in Paradise are unfatigued. And if she still does not know what it is she wants to solve, she has only to read on. The Crotona Park Branch is as paradisal here as it was on earth. She reads anthropology, zoology, physical chemistry, philosophy (in the green air of heaven Kant and Nietzsche together fall into crystal splinters). The New Books section is peerless: she will learn about the linkages of genes, about quarks, about primate sign language, theories of the origins of the races, religions of ancient civilizations, what Stonehenge meant. Puttermesser will read Non-Fiction into eternity; and there is still time for Fiction! Eden is equipped above all with timelessness, so Puttermesser will read at last all of Balzac, all of Dickens, all of Turgenev and Dostoevski (her mortal self has already read all of Tolstoy and George Eliot); at last Puttermesser will read *Kristin Lavransdatter* and the stupendous trilogy of Dmitri Merezhkovski, she will read *The Magic Mountain* and the whole *Faerie Queene* and every line of *The Ring and the Book*, she will read a biography of Beatrix Potter and one of Walter Scott in many entrancing volumes and one of Lytton Strachey, at last, at last! In Eden insatiable Puttermesser will be nourished, if not glutted. She will study Roman law, the more arcane varieties of higher mathematics, the nuclear composition of the stars, what happened to the Monophysites, Chinese history, Russian, and Icelandic.

But meanwhile, still alive, not yet translated upward, her days given over to the shadow reign of a playboy Commissioner, Puttermesser was learning only Hebrew.

Twice a week, at night (it seemed), she went to Uncle Zindel for a lesson. Where the bus ran through peeling neighborhoods the trolley tracks sometimes shone up through a broken smother of asphalt, like weeds wanting renewal. From childhood Puttermesser remembered how trolley days were better days: in summer the cars banged along, self-contained little carnivals, with open wire-mesh sides sucking in hot winds, the passengers serenely jogging on the seats. Not so this bus, closed like a capsule against the slum.

The old man, Zindel the Stingy, hung on to life among the cooking smells of Spanish-speaking blacks. Puttermesser walked up three flights of steps and leaned against the crooked door, waiting for the former shammes with his little sack. Each evening Zindel brought up a single egg from the Cuban grocery. He boiled it while Puttermesser sat with her primer.

"You should go downtown," the shammes said, "where they got regular language factories. Berlitz. N.Y.U. They even got an *ulpan*, like in Israel."

"You're good enough," Puttermesser said. "You know everything they know."

"And something more also. Why you don't live downtown, on the East Side, fancy?"

"The rent is too much, I inherited your stinginess."

"And such a name. A nice young fellow meets such a name, he laughs. You should change it to something different, lovely, nice. Shapiro, Levine. Cohen, Goldweiss, Blumenthal. I don't say make it *different*, who needs Adams, who needs McKee, I say make it a name not a joke. Your father gave you a bad present with it. For a young girl, Butterknife!"

"I'll change it to Margarine-messer."

"Never mind the ha-ha. *My* father, what was your great-great-grandfather, didn't allow a knife to the table Friday night. When it came to *kiddush*—knifes off! All knifes! On Sabbath an instrument, a blade? On Sabbath a weapon? A point? An edge? What makes bleeding among mankind? What makes war? Knifes! No knifes! Off! A clean table! And something else you'll notice. By us we got only *messer*, you follow? By them they got sword, they got lance, they got halberd. Go to the dictionary, I went once. So help me, what don't one of them knights carry? Look up in the book, you'll see halberd, you'll see cutlass, pike, rapier, foil, ten dozen more. By us a pike is a fish. Not to mention what nowadays they got— bayonet stuck on the gun, who knows what else the poor soldier got to carry in the pocket. Maybe a dagger same as a pirate. But by us—what we got? A *messer! Puttermesser*, you slice off a piece butter, you cut to live, not to kill. A name of honor, you follow? Still, for a young girl—"

"Uncle Zindel, I'm past thirty."

Uncle Zindel blinked lids like insect's wings, translucent. He saw her voyaging, voyaging. The wings of his eyes shadowed the Galilee. They moved over the Tomb of the Patriarchs. A tear for the tears of Mother Rachel rode on his nose. "Your mother knows you're going? Alone on an airplane, such a young girl? You wrote her?"

"I wrote her, Uncle Zindel. I'm not flying anywhere."

"By sea is also danger. What Mama figures, in Miami who is there? The dead and dying. In Israel you'll meet someone. You'll marry, you'll settle there. What's the difference, these days, modern times, quick travel—"

Uncle Zindel's egg was ready, hard-boiled. The shammes tapped it and the shell came off raggedly. Puttermesser consulted the alphabet: *aleph, beys, gimel*; she was not going to Israel, she had business in the Municipal Building. Uncle Zindel, chewing, began finally to teach: "First see how a *gimel* and which way a *zayen*. Twins, but one kicks a leg left, one right. You got to practice the difference. If legs don't work, think pregnant bellies. Mrs. *Zayen* pregnant in one direction, Mrs. *Gimel* in the other. Together they give birth to *gez*, which means what you cut off. A night for knifes! Listen, going home from here you should be extra careful tonight. Martinez, the upstairs not the next door, her daughter they mugged and they took."

The shammes chewed, and under his jaws Puttermesser's head bent, practicing the bellies of the holy letters.

Stop. Stop, stop! Puttermesser's biographer, stop! Disengage, please. Though it is true that biographies are invented, not recorded, here you invent too much. A symbol is allowed, but not a whole scene: do not accommodate too obsequiously to Puttermesser's romance. Having not much imagination, she is literal with what she has. Uncle Zindel lies under the earth of Staten Island. Puttermesser has never had a conversation with him; he died four years before her birth. He is all legend: Zindel the Stingy, who even in *gan eydn* rather than eat will store apples until they rot. Zindel the Unripe. Why must Puttermesser fall into so poignant a fever over the cracked phrases of a shammes of a torn-down shul?

(The shul was not torn down, neither was it abandoned. It disintegrated. Crumb by crumb it vanished. Stones took some of the windows. There were no pews, only wooden folding chairs. Little by little these turned into sticks. The prayer books began to flake: the bindings flaked, the glue came unstuck in small brown flakes, the leaves grew brittle and flaked into confetti. The congregation too began to flake off—the women first, wife after wife after wife, each one a pearl and a consolation, until there they stand, the widowers, frail, gazing, palsy-struck. Alone and in terror. Golden Agers, Senior Citizens! And finally they too flake away, the shammes among them. The shul becomes a wisp, a straw, a feather, a hair.)

But Puttermesser must claim an ancestor. She demands connection—surely a Jew must own a past. Poor Puttermesser has found herself in the world without a past. Her mother was born into the din of Madison Street and was taken up to the hullabaloo of Harlem at an early age. Her father is nearly a Yankee: his father gave up peddling to captain a dry-goods store in Providence, Rhode Island. In summer he sold captain's hats, and wore one in all his photographs. Of the world that was, there is only this single grain of memory: that once an old man, Puttermesser's mother's uncle, kept his pants up with a rope belt, was called Zindel, lived without a wife, ate frugally, knew the holy letters, died with thorny English a wilderness between his gums. To him Puttermesser clings. America is a blank, and Uncle Zindel is all her ancestry. Unironic, unimaginative, her plain but stringent mind strains beyond the parents—what did they have? Only day-by-day in their lives, coffee in the morning, washing underwear, occasionally a trip to the beach. Blank. What did they know? Everything from the movies; something—scraps—from the newspaper. Blank.

Behind the parents, beyond and before them, things teem. In old photographs of the Jewish East Side, Puttermesser sees the teeming. She sees a long coat. She sees a woman pressing onions from a pushcart. She sees a tiny child with a finger in its mouth who will become a judge.

Past the judge, beyond and behind him, something more is teeming. But this Puttermesser cannot see. The towns, the little towns. Zindel born into a flat-roofed house a modest distance from a stream.

What can Puttermesser do? She began life as the child of an anti-Semite. Her father would not eat kosher meat—it was, he said, too tough. He had no superstitions. He wore the mother down, she went to the regular meat market at last.

The scene with Uncle Zindel did not occur. How Puttermesser loved the voice of Zindel in the scene that did not occur!

(He is under the ground. The cemetery is a teeming city of toy skyscrapers shouldering each other. Born into a wooden house, Zindel now has a flat stone roof. Who buried him? Strangers from the *landsmanshaft* society. Who said a word for him? No one. Who remembers him now?)

Puttermesser does not remember Uncle Zindel; Puttermesser's mother does not remember him. A name in the dead grandmother's mouth. Her parents have no ancestry. Therefore Puttermesser rejoices in the cadences of Uncle Zindel's voice above the Cuban grocery. Uncle Zindel, when alive, distrusted the building of Tel Aviv because he was practical, Messiah was not imminent. But now, in the scene that did not occur, how naturally he supposes Puttermesser will journey to a sliver of earth in the Middle East, surrounded by knives, missiles, bazookas!

The scene with Uncle Zindel did not occur. It could not occur because, though Puttermesser dares to posit her ancestry, we may not. Puttermesser is not to be examined as an artifact but as an essence. Who made her? No one cares. Puttermesser is henceforth to be presented as given. Put her back into Receipts and Disbursements, among office Jews and patronage collectors. While winter dusk blackens the Brooklyn Bridge, let us hear her opinion about the taxation of exempt properties. The bridge is not the harp Hart Crane said it was in his poem. Its staves are prison bars. The women clerks, Yefimova, Korolova, Akulova, Arkhipova, Izrailova, are on Kolpachni Street, but the vainglorious General Viryein is not. He is on Ogaryova Street. Joel Zaretsky's ex-wife is barren. The Commissioner puts on his tennis sneakers. He telephones. Mr. Fiore, the courtly secret mayor behind the Mayor, also telephones. Hey! Puttermesser's biographer! What will you do with her now?

Shots

I came to photography as I came to infatuation—with no special talent for it, and with no point of view. Taking pictures —when *I* take them, I mean—has nothing to do with art and less to do with reality. I'm blind to what intelligent people call "composition," I revile every emanation of "grain," and any drag through a gallery makes me want to die. As for the camera as *machine*—well, I know the hole I have to look through, and I know how to press down with my finger. The rest is thingamajig. What brought me to my ingenious profession was no idea of the Photograph as successor to the Painting, and no pleasure in darkrooms, or in any accumulation of clanking detritus.

Call it necrophilia. I have fallen in love with corpses. Dead faces draw me. I'm uninformed about the history of photography—1832, the daguerreotype, mercury vapor; what an annoyance that so blatant a thing as picture-taking is considered worth applying a history to!—except to understand how long a past the camera has, measured by a century-old length of a woman's skirt. People talk of inventing a time machine, as if it hadn't already been invented in the box and shutter. I have been ravished by the last century's faces, now motes in their graves—such lost eyes, and noses, and mouths, and earlobes, and dress-collars: my own eyes soak these up; I can never leave off looking at anything brown and brittle and old and decaying at the edges.

The autumn I was eleven I found the Brown Girl. She was under a mound of chestnut-littered leaves near five tall trash barrels in a corner of the yard behind the Home for the Elderly Female Ill. Though the old-lady inmates were kept confined to a high balcony above the browning grass of their bleak overgrown yard, occasionally I would see some witless half-bald refugee shuffling through a weed-sea with stockings rolled midway down a sinewy blue calf engraved by a knotted garter. They scared me to death, these sticks and twigs of brainless ancients, rattling their china teeth and howling at me in foreign tongues, rolling the bright gems of their mad old eyes inside their nearly visible crania. I used to imagine that if one of these fearful witches could just somehow get beyond the gate, she would spill off garters and fake teeth and rheumy eye-whites and bad smells and stupid matted old flesh, and begin to bloom all plump and glowing and ripe again: Shangri-La in reverse.

What gave me this imagining was the Brown Girl. Any one of these pitiful decaying sacks might once have been the Brown Girl. If only someone had shot a kind of halt-arrow through the young nipples of the Brown Girl at the crest of her years, if only she had been halted, arrested, stayed in her ripeness and savor!

The Brown Girl lived. She lay in a pile of albums dumped into the leaves. It seemed there were hundreds of her: a girl in a dress that dropped to the buttons of her shoes, with an arched bosom and a hint of bustle, and a face mysteriously shut: you never once saw her teeth, you never once saw the lips in anything like the hope of a smile; laughter was out of the question. A grave girl; a sepia girl; a girl as brown as the ground. She must have had her sorrows.

Gradually (to my eyes suddenly) I saw her age. It wasn't that the plain sad big-nosed face altered: no crinkles at the lids, no grooves digging out a distinct little parallelogram from nostril-sides to mouth-ends—or, if these were in sight, they weren't what I noticed. The face faded out—became not there. The woman turned to ghost. The ghost wore different clothes now, too familiar to gape at. The fingers were ringless. The eyes whitened off. Somehow for this melancholy spinster's sake the first rule of the box camera was always being violated: not to put the sun behind your subject. A vast blurred drowning orb of sun flooded massively, habitually down from the upper right corner of her picture. Whoever photographed her, over years and years and years, meant to obliterate her. But I knew it was no sun-bleach that conspired to efface her. What I was seeing—what I *had* seen—was time. And not time on the move, either, the illusion of stories and movies. What I had seen was time as stasis, time at the standstill, time at the fix; the time (though I hadn't yet reached it in school) of Keats's Grecian urn. The face faded out because death was coming: death the changer, the collapser, the witherer; death the bleacher, blancher, whitener.

The truth is, I'm looked on as a close-mouthed professional, serious about my trade, who intends to shut up and keep secrets when necessary. I repel all "technical" questions—if someone wants to discuss the make of my camera (it's Japanese), or my favorite lens, or some trick I might have in developing, or what grade of paper I like, I'll stare her down. Moonings on Minor White's theories I regard as absolutely demeaning. I have a grasp on what I am about, and it isn't any of that.

What it is, is the Brown Girl. I kept her. I kept her, I mean, in a pocket of my mind (and one of her pictures in the pocket of my blouse); I kept her because she was dead. What I expect you to take from this is that I *could* keep her *even though* she was dead. I wasn't infatuated by her (not that she was the wrong sex: infatuation, like any passion of recognition, neglects gender); she was too oppressed and brown and quiet for that. But it was she who gave me the miraculous hint: a hint derived from no science of mechanics or physics, a rapturous hint on the other side of art, beyond metaphor, deep in the wonderfully literal. What she made me see was that if she wasn't a girl any more, if she wasn't a woman any more, if she was very likely not even a member of the elderly female ill any more (by the time her photos fell among the leaves, how long had she been lying under them?), still I *had* her, actually and physically and with the certainty of simple truth. I could keep her, just as she used to be, because someone had once looked through the bunghole of a box and clicked off a lever. Whoever had desultorily drowned her in too much sun had anyhow given her a monument two inches wide and three inches long. What happened then was here now. I had it in the pocket of my blouse.

Knowing this—that now will become then, that huge will turn little—doesn't cure. I walk around the wet streets with a historian now, a tenured professor of South American history: he doesn't like to go home to his wife. Somehow it always rains when we meet, and it's Sam's big blue umbrella, with a wooden horse's head for a handle, that preoccupies me this instant. Which is strange: he hasn't owned it for a whole year. It was left in a yellow garish coffee shop on the night side of a street you couldn't trust, and when Sam went back, only ten minutes later, to retrieve it, of course it wasn't there.

At that time I didn't care about one thing in Sam's mind. I had to follow him, on assignment, all through a course of some public symposia he was chairing. We had—temporarily —the same employer. His college was setting up a glossy little booklet for the State Department to win South American friends with: I had to shoot Sam on the podium with Uruguayans, Sam on the podium with Brazilians, Sam on the podium with Peruvians, and so forth. It was a lackluster job—I had just come, not so long ago, from photographing an intergalactic physicist whose bravest hope was the invention of an alphabet to shoot into the kindergartens of the cosmos—so it was no trouble at all not to listen to the speeches while I shot the principals. Half the speeches were in Portuguese or Spanish, and if you wanted to you could put on earphones anywhere in the hall and hear a simultaneous translation. The translator sat at the squat end of the long symposium table up on the stage with Sam and the others, but kept his microphone oddly close to his lips, like a kiss, sweat sliding and gleaming along his neck—it seemed he was tormented by that bifurcated concentration. His suffering attracted me. He didn't count as one of the principals—the celebrity of the day (now it was night, the last of the dark raining afternoon) was the vice-consul of Chile—but I shot him anyhow, for my own reasons: I liked the look of that shining sweat on his bulging Adam's apple. I calculated my aim (I'm very fast at this), shot once, shot again, and was amazed to see blood spring out of a hole in his neck. The audience fell apart—it was like watching an anthill after you've kicked into it; there was a spaghetti of wires and police; the simultaneous translator was dead. It made you listen for the simultaneous silence of the principal speaker, but the Chilean vice-consul only swerved his syllables into shrieks, with his coat over his head; he was walked away in a tremor between two colleagues suddenly sprouting guns. A mob of detectives took away my film; it was all I could do to keep them from arresting my camera. I went straight to Sam —it was his show—to complain. "That's *film* in there, not bullets." "It's evidence now," Sam said. "Who wanted to do that?" I said. "God knows," Sam said; "they didn't do what they wanted anyhow," and offered six political possibilities, each of which made it seem worthwhile for someone to do away with the Chilean vice-consul. He found his umbrella under the table and steered me out. The rain had a merciless wind in it, and every glassy sweep of it sent fountains spitting upward from the pavement. We stood for a while under his umbrella (he gripping the horse's head hard enough to whiten his knuckles) and watched them carry the simultaneous translator out. He was alone on a stretcher; his duality was done, his job as surrogate consummated. I reflected how quickly vertical becomes horizontal. "You knew him," I said.

"Only in a public way. He's been part of all these meetings."

"So have I," I said.

"I've watched you watching me."

I resisted this. "That's professional watching. It's more like stalking. I always stalk a bit before I shoot."

"You talk like a terrorist," Sam said, and began a history of South American conspiracy, which group was aligned with whom, who gave asylum, who withheld it, who the Chilean vice-consul's intimates across several borders were, at this instant plotting vengeance. He had exactly the kind of mentality —cumulative, analytical—I least admired, but since he also had the only umbrella in sight, I stuck with him. He was more interested in political factionalism—he had to get everything

sorted out, and his fascination seemed to be with the victims—
than in his having just sat two feet from a murder. "My God,"
I said finally, "doesn't the power of inaccuracy impress you? It
could've been you on that stretcher."

"I don't suppose *you* ever miss your target," he said.

"No," I said, "but I don't shoot to kill."

"Then you're not one of those who want to change the
world," he said, and I could smell in this the odor of his melancholy. He was a melancholic and an egotist; this made me a
bit more attentive. His umbrella, it appeared, was going to
pilot him around for miles and miles; I went along as passen-
ger. We turned at last into a coffee shop—this wasn't the place
he lost the horse's head in—and then turned out again, heated
up, ready for more weather. "Don't you ever go home?" I
asked him.

"Don't you?"

"I live alone."

"I don't. I hate my life," he said.

"I don't blame you. You've stuffed it up with South American facts."

"Would you like North American facts better?"

"I can't take life in whole continents," I protested.

"The thing about taking it in continents is that you don't
have to take it face by face."

"The faces are the best part."

"Some are the worst," Sam said.

I looked into his; he seemed a victim of factionalism himself, as if you become what you study. He had rather ferocious
eyes, much too shiny, like something boiling in a pot—the
ferocity made you think them black, but really they were pale
—and black ripe rippled hair and unblemished orderly teeth,
not white but near-white. "Which faces are the worst?"

"Now I'll go home," he said.

The murder had cut short the series of symposia; the South

Americans scattered, which was too bad—they were Sam's source of vitality. But it never occurred to either of us that we might not meet again officially, and often enough we did—he on a platform, myself with camera. Whether this meant that all the magazine people I knew—the ones who were commissioning my pictures—were all at once developing a fevered concern for South American affairs (more likely it was for terrorism) is a boring question. I know I wasn't. I never wanted to listen to Sam on the subjects he was expert in, and I never did. I only caught what I thought of as their "moans"— impure and simmering and winnowing and sad. The sounds that came through his microphone were always intensely public: he was, his audience maintained—loyalists, they trotted after him from speech to speech—a marvelous generalist. He could go from predicting the demand for bauxite to tracing migrations of Indian populations, all in a single stanza. He could connect disparate packets of contemporary information with a linking historic insight that took your breath away. He was a very, very good public lecturer; all his claque said so. He could manage to make anyone (or everyone but me) care about South America. Still, I had a little trick in my head as he declaimed and as I popped my flashbulbs, not always at him— more often at the distinguished sponsors of the event. I could tell they were distinguished from the way they dragged me up to the dais to photograph them—it showed how important they were. Sometimes they wanted to be photographed just before Sam began, and sometimes, with their arms around him, when he was just finished, themselves grinning into Sam's applause. All the while I kept the little trick going.

The little trick was this: whatever he said that was vast and public and South American, I would simultaneously translate (I hoped I wouldn't be gunned down for it) into everything private and personal and secret. This required me to listen shrewdly to the moan behind the words—I had to blot out the words for the sake of the tune. Sometimes the tune would be civil or sweet or almost jolly—especially if he happened to get a look at me before he ascended to his lectern—but mainly it would be narrow and drab and resigned. I knew he had a wife, but I was already thirty-six, and who didn't have a wife by then? I wasn't likely to run into them if they didn't. Bachelors wouldn't be where I had to go, particularly not in public halls gaping at the per capita income of the interior villages of the Andes, or the future of Venezuelan oil, or the fortunes of the last Paraguayan bean crop, or the differences between the centrist parties in Bolivia and Colombia, or whatever it was that kept Sam ladling away at his tedious stew. I drilled through all these sober-shelled facts into their echoing gloomy melodies: and the sorrowful sounds I unlocked from their casings—it was like breaking open a stone and finding the music of the earth's wild core boiling inside—came down to the wife, the wife, the wife. That was the tune Sam was moaning all the while: wife wife wife. He didn't like her. He wasn't happy with her. His whole life was wrong. He was a dead man. If I thought I'd seen a dead man when they took that poor fellow out on that stretcher, I was stupidly mistaken; *he* was ten times deader than that. If the terrorist who couldn't shoot straight had shot *him* instead, he couldn't be more riddled with gunshot than he was this minute—he was smoking with his own death.

In the yellow garish coffee shop he went on about his wife —he shouldn't be telling me all this, my God, what the hell did he think he was doing; he was a fool; he was a cliché; he was out of a cartoon or an awful play; he was an embarrassment to himself and to me. It was either a trance or a seizure. And then he forgot his umbrella, and ran back after it, and it was gone. It wouldn't have had, necessarily, to be a desperate thief who stole his horse's head that night; it might easily have been a nice middle-class person like ourselves. A nice middle-class person especially would have hated to be out in such a drenching without a shred of defense overhead—Sam charged on into gales of cold rain, and made me charge onward too: for the first time he had me by the hand. I wouldn't let him keep it, though—I had to bundle my camera under my coat.

"How long are we going to walk in this?" I said.

"We'll walk and walk."

"I've got to go home or I'll soak my equipment," I complained.

"I'm not going home."

"Don't you ever go home?"

"My whole life is wrong," he said.

We spilled ourselves into another coffee place and sat there till closing. My shoes were seeping and seeping. He explained Verity: "I admire her," he said. "I esteem her, you wouldn't believe how I esteem that woman. She's a beautiful mother. She's strong and she's bright and she's independent and there's nothing she can't do."

"Now tell her good points," I said.

"She can fix a car. She always fixes the car. Puts her head into the hood and fixes it. She builds furniture. We live in a madhouse of excess property—she built every stick of it. She saws like a madwoman. She *sews* like a madwoman—I don't mean just *clothes*. She sews her own clothes and the girls' clothes too. What I mean is she *sews*—bedspreads and curtains and upholstery, even *car* upholstery. And she's got a whole budding career of her own. I've made her sound like a bull, but she's really very delicate at whatever she does—she does plates, you know."

"License plates?"

"She's done *some* metalwork—her minor was metallurgy—but what I'm talking about is ceramics. Porcelain. She does painted platters and pots and pitchers and sells them to Bloomingdale's."

"She's terrific," I said.

"She's terrific," he agreed. "There's nothing she can't do."

"Cook?"

"My God, *cook*," he said. "French, Italian, Indian, whatever you want. And bakes. Pastries, the difficult stuff, crusts made of cloud. She's a domestic genius. We have this big harp —hell, it was busted, a skeleton in a junk shop, so she bought it cheap and repaired it—she plays it like an angel. You think you're in heaven inside that hell. She plays the piano, too— classics, ragtime, rock. She's got a pretty nice singing voice. She's good at basketball—she practically never misses a shot. Don't ask me again if I admire her."

I asked him again if he admired her.

"I'm on my knees," he groaned. "She's a goddamn goddess. She's powerful and autonomous and a goddamn genius. Christ," he said, "I hate my life."

"If I had someone like that at home," I said, "I'd never be out in the rain."

"She could abolish the weather if she wanted to, only she doesn't want to. She has a terrific will."

I thought this over and was surprised by my sincerity: "You ought to go home," I told him.

"Let's walk."

After that we met more or less on purpose. The South American fad wore off—there was a let-up in guerrilla activity down there—and it got harder to find him in public halls, so I went up to his college now and then and sat in on his classes, and afterward, rain or shine, but mostly rain, we walked. He told me about his daughters—one of them was nearly as terrific as Verity herself—and we walked with our arms hooked. "Is something happening here?" I inquired. "Nothing will ever happen here," he said. We had a friend in common, the editor who'd assigned me to photographing that intergalactic physicist I've mentioned; it turned out we were asked, Sam with

Verity, myself as usual, to the editor's party, in honor of the editor's ascension. There were some things the editor hadn't done which added immensely to his glory; and because of all the things he hadn't done they were making him vice-chancellor of Sam's college. I did justice to those illustrious gaps and omissions: I took the host, now majestic, and his wife, their children, their gerbil, their maid. I shot them embedded in their guests. I dropped all those pictures behind me like autumn leaves. I hadn't brought my usual Japanese spy, you see; I'd carried along a tacky Polaroid instead—instant development, a detective story without a detective, ah, I disliked that idea, but the evening needed its jester. I aimed and shot, aimed and shot, handing out portraits deciduously. Verity had her eye on all this promiscuity; she was blond and capacious and maybe capricious; she seemed without harm and without mercy.

"You're the one who shot the simultaneous translator," she said.

"Judicial evidence," I replied.

"Now let me," she said, "ask you something about your trade. In photography, do you consistently get what you expect?"

I said: "It's the same as life."

Verity expressed herself: "The viewfinder, the viewfinder!"

"I always look through that first," I admitted.

"And then do you get what you see? I mean can you predict exactly, or are you always surprised by what comes out?"

"I can never predict," I told her, "but I'm never surprised."

"That's fatalism," Verity said. Her voice was an iron arrow; she put her forefinger into my cheek as humbly as a bride. "Talk about shots, here's a parting one. You take a shot at Sam, no expectations. He's not like life. He's safe. He's *good*."

He was safe and he was good: Sam the man of virtue. She knew everything exactly, even when everything was nothing she knew it exactly, she was without any fear at all; jealousy wasn't in her picture; she was more virtuous than he was, she was big, she had her great engine, she was her own cargo. And you see what it is with infatuation: it comes on you as quick as a knife. It's a bullet in the neck. It gets you from the outside. One moment you're in your prime of health, the next you're in anguish. Until then—until I had the chance to see for myself how clear and proud his wife was—Sam was an entertainment, not so entertaining after all. Verity was the Cupid of the thing, Verity's confidence the iron arrow that dragged me down. She had her big foot on her sour catch. I saw in her glow, in her sureness, in her pride, in her tall ship's prow of certitude, the plausibility of everything she knew: he'd have to go home in the end.

But the end's always at the end; in the meantime there's the meantime.

How to give over these middle parts? I couldn't see what I looked like, from then on, to Sam: all the same I had my automatic intelligence—light acting on a treated film. I was treated enough; Verity had daubed me. Since I was soaked in her solution, infatuation took, with me, a mechanical form—if you didn't know how mechanical it was, you would have imagined it was sly. I could listen now to everything Sam said. Without warning, I could *follow* him; I discovered myself in the act of wanting more. I woke up one morning in a fit of curiosity about the quantity of anthracite exports on the Brazilian littoral. I rooted in hard-to-find volumes of Bolívar's addresses. I penetrated the duskier hells of the public library and boned up on every banana republic within reach. It was astounding: all at once, and for no reason—I mean for *the* reason—Sam interested me. It was like walking on the lining of his brain.

On the South American issue he was dense as a statue. He had never noticed that I hadn't paid attention to his subject before; he didn't notice that I was attentive now. His premise was that everyone alive without exception was all the time infatuated with the former Spanish Empire. On *my* subject, though, Sam was trying; it was because of Verity; she had made him ambitious to improve himself with me.

"Verity saw at that party," he said, "that you had the kind of camera that gets you the picture right away."

"Not exactly right away. You have to wait a minute," I corrected.

"Why don't you use a camera like that all the time? It's magic. It's like a miracle."

"Practical reasons of the trade. The farther you are from having what you think you want, the more likely you are to get it. It's just that you have to wait. You really have to *wait*. What's important is the waiting."

Sam didn't get it. "But it's *chemistry*. The image is already on the film. It's the same image one minute later or two months later."

"You're too miracle-minded even for a historian," I admonished him. "It's not like that at all. If you have a change of heart between shooting your picture and taking it out of the developer, the picture changes too." I wanted to explain to him how, between the exposure and the solution, history comes into being, but telling that would make me bleed, like a bullet in the neck, so I said instead, "Photography is *literal*. It gets what's *there*."

Meanwhile the rain is raining on Sam and me. We meet in daylight now, and invent our own occasions. We hold hands, we hook arms, we walk through the park. There is a mole on his knuckle which has attached itself to my breathing; my lungs grasp all the air they can. I want to lay my tears on the hairs of his fingers. Because of the rain, the daylight is more like twilight; in this perpetual half of dusk, the sidewalks a kind of blackened purple, like fallen plums, we talk about the past and the future of the South American continent. Verity is in her house. I leave my camera behind too. Our faces are rivers, we walk without an umbrella, the leaves splash. When I can't find Sam on my own, I telephone Verity; she stops the motor of her sewing machine and promises to give him the message when he returns. He comes flying out to meet me, straight from his Committee on Inter-American Conditions; I'm practically a colleague now, and a pleasure to talk to about Ecuadorian peonage. He tells me he's never had a mistress and never will; his wife is too remarkable. I ask him whether he's ever walked in a summer rain this way with anyone else. He admits he has; he admits it hasn't lasted. "The rain hasn't lasted? Or the feeling?" He forgets to answer. I remember that *he* is only interested; it's I who feel. We talk some more about the native religions still hiding out in the pampas; we talk about the Jewish gauchos in nineteenth-century Argentina. He takes it all for granted. He doesn't realize how hard I've had to study. A big leaf like a pitcher overturns itself all over our heads, and we make a joke about Ponce de León and the Fountain of Youth. I ask him then if he'll let me take his picture in the park, under a dripping linden tree, in a dangerous path, so that I can keep him forever, in case it doesn't last.

I see that he doesn't understand. He doesn't understand: unlike me, he's not under any special spell, he's not in thrall to any cult. That's the rub always—infatuation's unilateral or it doesn't count as real. I think he loves me—he may even be "in love"—but he's not caught like me. He'd never trace my life over as I've traced over his brain waves. He asks me why I want to shoot him under the linden tree. I tell him the truth I took from his wife: virtue ravishes me. I want to keep its portrait. I am silent about the orphaned moment we're living in now, how it will leave us. I feel, I feel our pathos. We are virtue's orphans. The tree's green shoots are fleeting; all green corrupts to brown. Sam denies that he's a man of virtue. It's only his guilt about Verity: she's too terrific to betray.

He consents to having his picture taken in the sopping park if I agree to go home with him afterward.

I say in my amazement, "I can't go home with you. She's *there*."

"She's always there."

"Then how can I go home with you?"

"You have to *see*. It's all been too obscure. I want you to know what I know."

"I know it, you've told me. You've told and told."

"You have to get the smell of it. Where I am and how I live. Otherwise you won't believe in it. You won't know it," he insists. "Such cozy endurances."

"You endure them," I said.

"Yesterday," he said, "she brought home a box of old clothes from the Salvation Army. From a thrift shop. From an old people's home, who knows where she got it from. Pile of rags. She's going to sew them into God's bright ribbons. A patchwork quilt. She'll spin straw into gold, you'll see."

"She's terrific."

"She's a terrific wife," he says.

We walk to my place, pick up my camera—I stop to grab my light meter for the rain's sake—and walk crosstown to the park again. I shoot Sam, the man of virtue, under the dripping linden tree. Although I am using my regular equipment, it seems to me the picture's finished on the spot. It's as if I roll it out and fix it then and there. Sam has got his back against the bark, and all the little wet leaves lick down over his bumpy hair. He resembles a Greek runner resting. His face is dappled by all those heart-shaped leaves, and I know that all the rest of my life I'll regret not having shot him in the open, in a field. But my wish for now is to speckle him and see him darkle under the rainy shade of a tree. It comes to me that my desire —oh, my desire! it stings me in the neck—is just now not even for Sam's face: it's for the transitoriness of these thin vulnerable leaves, with their piteous veins turned upward toward a faintness of liverish light.

We walk the thirty-one blocks, in the quickening rain, to his place. It's only a four-room apartment, but Verity's made a palace of it. Everything plain is converted into a sweetness, a furriness, a thickness of excess. She weaves, she knits. She's an immense spider building out of her craw. The floors are piled with rugs she's woven, the chairs with throws she's knit. She's cemented up a handy little fireplace without a flue; it really works, and on a principle she invented herself. She's carpentered all the bookcases—I catch the titles of the four books Sam's written; he's a dignitary and a scholar, after all—and overhead there wafts and dazzles the royal chandelier she found in the gutter and refurbished. Each prism slid through her polishing and perfecting fingers. Verity resurrects, Verity's terrific—you can't avoid thinking it. She's got her big shoulders mounted over her sewing machine in the corner of the living room, hemming brown squares. "It's weird, you wouldn't believe it," she says, "*all* the stuff in this box they gave me is brown. It's good rich fabric, though—a whole load of clothes from dead nuns. You know what happened? A convent dissolved, the young nuns broke their vows and ran to get married."

"That's *your* story," Sam says.

Verity calls her daughter—only one of the girls is at home, the other is away at college. Clearly this one isn't the daughter that's so much like Verity. She has a solemn hard flank of cheek, and no conversation. She carries out a plate of sliced honey cake and three cups of tea; then she hides herself in her bedroom. A radio is in there; gilded waves of Bach tremble out of it. I look around for Verity's harp.

"Hey, let's dress you up," Verity says out of her teacup;

she's already downed a quantity of cake. "There's stuff in that box that would just fit you. You've got a waist like our girls. I wish *I* had a waist like that." I protest; I tell her it's too silly. Sam smolders with his sour satisfaction, and she churns her palms inside the box like a pair of oars. She pulls out a long skirt, and a blouse called a bodice, and another blouse to wear under that, with long sleeves. Sam pokes my spine and nudges me into the girl's bedroom, where there's a tall mirror screwed into the back of the door. I look at myself.

"Period piece!" says Verity.

I'm all in brown, as brown as leaves. The huge high harp, not gold as I imagined it but ivory, is along the wall behind me. I believe everything Sam has told about the conquistadores. I believe everything he's told about Verity. He's a camera who never lies. His wet hair is black as olives. He belongs to his wife, who's terrific. She's put a nun's bonnet on herself. She has an old-fashioned sense of fun—the words come to me out of, I think, Louisa May Alcott: she likes costume and dress-up. Soon she will have us guessing riddles and playing charades. They are a virtuous and wholesome family. The daughter, though her look is bone, is fond of Bach; no junk music in such a household. They are sweeter than the whole world outside. When Sam is absent the mother and her daughter climb like kittens into a knitted muff.

I shoot Verity wearing the nun's bonnet.

"Look at *you!*" she cries.

I return to the mirror to see. I am grave; I have no smile. My face is mysteriously shut. I'm suffering. Lovesick and dreamsick, I'm dreaming of my desire. I am already thirty-six years old, tomorrow I will be forty-eight years old, and a crafty parallelogram begins to frame the space between my nose and mouth. My features are very distinct—I will live for years and years before they slide out of the mirror. I'm the Brown Girl in the pocket of my blouse. I reek of history. If, this minute, I could glide into a chemical solution, as if in a gondola, splashed all over and streaming with wet silver, would the mirror seize and fix me, like a photographic plate? I watch Sam's eyes, poached and pale and mottled with furious old civilizations, steaming hatred for his wife. I trip over the long drapery of my nun's hem. All the same I catch up my camera without dropping it—my ambassador of desire, my secret house with its single shutter, my chaste aperture, my dead infant, husband of my bosom. Their two heads, hers light, his black, negatives of each other, are caught side by side in their daughter's mirror. I shoot into their heads, the white harp behind. Now they are exposed. Now they will stick forever.

From a Refugee's Notebook

Redactor's Comment: These fragments, together with the above unprepossessing title, were found (in a purple-covered spiral tablet of the kind used by university students of an earlier generation and in another country) behind a mirror in a vacant room-for-rent on West 106th Street, New York City. The author, of European or perhaps South American origin, remains unidentified.

I. FREUD'S ROOM

Not long ago they turned Freud's house in Vienna into a museum, but few visitors come. It is even hard to know it is there: the big hotels don't list it on their bulletin boards, no one thinks of it as part of the tourist circuit. If you want to find it, the only place to ask is at the police station.

I have not been there myself (I do not go to any land which once suckled the Nazi boot), but I have dreamed over photographs of those small rooms where Sigmund Freud wrote his treatises and met with his patients and kept, in a glass case, his collection of ancient stone animals and carved figurines. There is a picture of Freud sitting at his desk, looking downward through dark-rimmed perfectly round lenses at a manuscript; behind him is the shining case with a good-sized camel, wood or stone, on top of it, and a great Grecian urn to the side. There are a wall of books, a vase of pussy willows, and on every shelf and surface cups, goblets, beasts, and hundreds of those strange little gods.

The museum, I suppose, is clear now of all that Egyptian debris, unless somehow it has all been brought back to fill the emptiness of the refugee's rooms.

In another of these famous photographs there is a curious juxtaposition. The picture is divided exactly in two by a lamp pole. On the left there is the crowd of stone godlets, on the right the couch on which Freud's patients lay during analysis. The wall behind the couch is covered by a Persian carpet hung in lieu of a tapestry; the couch itself is draped, in a heavy, ugly way, by another carpet hiding a hump of bolster beneath it and wearing a soft flat velveteen pillow as a kind of depressed beret. The very center of the picture is occupied by the low plush armchair in which Freud himself sat. The arms of the chair look worn, the whole small space seems cramped by so many objects, so many picture frames dangling in clumsy disorder up and down and across the wall behind the armchair and the couch. In one of the frames, under glass, the flanks of a greyhound dog glimmer. All this, of course, is what we have come to think of as Victorian clutter, and one pities the housemaid who came timidly in with her perilous duster. Yet if you take a second look, there is no clutter. Everything in the room is necessary: the couch and the gods. Even the slim dog who runs and yelps on the wall.

Especially the gods. The gods, the gods!

It is not the juxtaposition you suppose. What you are thinking is this: these primitive stone things, ranged like small determined marchers on shelves and tables (is it not amazing how many of them have one foot thrust forward, like the men who marched afterward in Vienna, or is it simply that the sculptor requires this posture for balance, else his god would shatter?)—these stone things, then, represent the deep primitive grain of the mind Freud sought. The woman or man on the couch was an archaeological enterprise—layer after layer to be spaded and sifted through, ever so delicately as archaeologists do, with feather brush, like the maid who slips in every morning to touch the top of each stone head with a sculptor's tender fear of despoiling the very matter the god-spirit has entrusted to him.

(The German word for matter is excellent, and illumines our English usage: *der Stoff*. Stuff. As in: the stuff of the universe. The wonder of the term is its thinginess. The awesome little gods in Freud's consulting room are matter, stuff, crumbs of rock; rubble.)

No, the juxtaposition I am thinking of is not merely the tangency of primitive with primitive. It is something else. The proliferation of gods, in mobs and bevies, the carpets with their diamond and flower figures, their languid tassels drooping down, the heavy figured table shawl with even longer fringes, over which a handful of gods blindly parade, the varnished brown wood frames, the vases curved and straight-sided, the libation cups standing dry, the burdensome tomes with their oppressive squatness mimicking pyramids—it is the room of a king.

The breath of this room drones with dreams of a king who lusts to become a god absolute as stone. The dreams that rise up from couch and armchair mix and braid in the air: the patient recounts her dream of a cat, signifying the grimness of a bad mother, and behind this dream, lurking in the doctor, is the doctor's dream. The gods walking over the long-fringed table shawl have chosen their king.

Respected reader: if I seem to be saying that Sigmund Freud wished to be a god, do not mistake me. I am no poet, and despise metaphors. I am a literal-minded person. I have no patience with figures of speech. Music is closed to me, and of art I have seen little. I have suffered the harsh life of a refugee and have made my living in bolts of cloth. I am familiar with texture: I can, with eyes shut, tell you which is rayon and which silk, which the genuine wool and which the synthetic, which pure nylon and which graduated toward cotton, which the coarse lace and which the fine. My whole bent is toward the tangible and the palpable. I know the difference between what is there and what is not there; between the empty and the full. I have nothing to do with make-believe.

I tell you that Sigmund Freud wished to become a god.

Some few men in history have wished it and would, but for mortality, have achieved it—some by tyranny: the Pharaohs indisputably, and also that Louis who was Sun King of France. Some by great victories: Napoleon and Hannibal. Some by chess: those world masters who murder in effigy the potent queens of their imaginings. Some by novel-writing: that conquistador Tolstoy who used only himself, costumed and dyed, under other names, and his aunties and his brothers and his poor wife Sonya (pragmatic and sensible like myself). Some by medicine and dentistry, wizardries of prosthesis and transplantation.

But others scheming to become gods utilize another resource altogether. Kings, generals, chess masters, surgeons, even those who wreak immense works of imagination—their resources are ultimately their sanity; their sobriety; their bourgeois probity. (Bourgeois? The sacred monarchs too? Yes; to live a decent life in dynastic Egypt, with food not likely to fester, clean drains, and comfortable beds, it was necessary to own ten thousand slaves.) The notion of the mad genius is a foolish and false commonplace. Ambition sniffs out the grain of logic and possibility. Genius summons up not grotesqueries but verisimilitudes: the lifelike, the anti-magical. Whoever seeks to become an earthly god must follow the earth itself.

Some few do not. At least two have not. The inventor of the

Sabbath—call him Moses if you wish—declared the cycle of the earth null. What do the birds, the worms their prey, the corn in the field, men and animals who sleep and wake up hungry, know of a Sabbath, this arbitrary call to make a stop in the diurnal rhythm, to move consciously apart from the natural progression of days? It is only God, standing apart from nature, who tells nature to cease, who causes miracles, who confounds logic.

After Moses, Freud. They are not alike. What the Sabbath and its emanations sought to suppress, Freud meant to reveal: everything barbarous and dreadful and veiled and terror-bearing: the very tooth and claw. What the roiling half-savage village Christianity of the Dark Ages called Hell, Freud called Id, which he similarly described as a "cauldron." And just as the village priest with a gift for the drama of fright peopled Hell with this and that demon, Beelzebub, Eblis, Apollyon, Mephisto, those curiously-named assistants or doubles of Satan, so Freud peopled the Unconscious with the devils of Id and Ego and Superego, potent dancing ghosts who cavort unrecorded in our anatomies while we pretend they are not there. And this too is to go against the diurnal rhythm of things. Nature does not stop to suspect itself of daily subterfuge. Inventing such a stop, Freud imposed on all our surface coherencies a Sabbath of the soul.

Which is to moon over the obvious: Freud was lured by what was clearly not "sane." The draw of the irrational has its own deep question: how much is research, how much search? Is the scientist, the intelligent physician, the skeptical philosopher who is attracted to the irrational, himself a rational being? How explain the attraction? I think of that majestic scholar of Jerusalem sitting in his university study composing, with bookish distance and objectivity, volume after volume on the history of Jewish mysticism . . . is there an objective "scientific interest" or is all interest a snare? And Freud: is the student of the dream-life—that subterranean grotto all drowned and darkling, torn with the fury of anguish and lust —is the student of the dream-life not himself a lovesick captive of it? Is the hidden cauldron not an enticement and a seduction to its inventor? Is the doctor of the Unconscious not likely to be devoured by his own creation, like that rabbi of Prague who constructed a golem?

Or, to say it even more terribly: it may be that the quarry is all the time in the pursuer.

[Here the first fragment ends.]

II. THE SEWING HAREMS

It was for a time the fashion on the planet Acirema for the more sophisticated females to form themselves into Sewing Harems. Each Sewing Harem would present itself for limited rental, in a body, to a rich businessman capable of housing it in a suitably gracious mansion or tasteful duplex apartment or roomy ranch or luxurious penthouse. Prices ran high. The typical Sewing Harem could be had for a little over seventy-five thousand dollars, but hiring one of these groups was splendidly prestigious, and was worth sacrificing foreign travel for, a new car, or even college for one's children.

What the Sewing Harems sewed was obvious. Do not visualize quilting bees, samplers, national flags.

What I have failed to mention so far is that the atmosphere of this planet contained a profusion of imperva molecules, which had the property of interacting with hormonal chemistry in such a way as to allow the women of that place to sew their own bodies with no anguish whatsoever. Imperva molecules had been present only since the last ice age, and their inherent volatility offered no guarantee that they could withstand the temperature assaults of the next ice age; but since no one was predicting a new ice age, and since the last one had been over for at least a hundred million years, no immediate atmospheric peril was anticipated.

Once rented, the Sewing Harem would incarcerate itself in

comfortable chambers, feast abundantly but privately, and rest prodigiously. After a day or so of hungerless inactivity, the sewing would begin.

There was considerable virtuosity in the style of stitches, but the most reliable, though not the most aesthetic, was the backstitch, which consists of two, sometimes three, running stitches, the final one repeated over upon itself. One woman would sew another, with the most cooperative cheerfulness imaginable, though occasionally an agile woman—an athlete or acrobat or dancer—managed, with fastidious poise, in exquisite position, to sew herself.

There was, as I have explained, no anguish in the flesh. Still, there was the conventional bleeding while the needle penetrated again and again, and the thread, whatever color was used, had to be tugged along swollen by wet blood, so that the whole length of it was finally dyed dark red. Healing took the usual week or so, and then the man who had leased the Sewing Harem was admitted to try whatever licentious pleasure his fancy and theirs could invent—except, of course, bodily entry. Inaccessibility increased wit, discrimination, maneuverability, and intellectuality on both sides.

The terms of the rental did not allow for snipping open stitches.

At the close of the rental period (between three and six months), a not insignificant number of the women would have become pregnant. How this could have happened I leave to the reader's nimble imagination, but surely in several instances stitches had been opened in defiance of contractual obligations, and perhaps even with the complicity and connivance of the women in question.

The terms of rental further stipulated that should any children be born to any of the women as a consequence of the activity of the leasing period, said children would be held in common by all the women: each one, equal with every other, would be designated as mother.

Now it should be immediately evident that all of this was far, far less than ordinary custom. The lighthearted hiring of Sewing Harems was practiced in a number of the great cities of that planet, but could be found hardly at all in the underdeveloped countries. The formation of Sewing Harems—or so it was charged by the Left and the Right—was the fad of the self-indulgent and the irrepressibly reckless. Not altogether so: since after the period of the lease expired, the members of each Sewing Harem, in their capacity as equal mothers, often attempted to remain together, and to continue as a serious social body, in order to raise its children intelligently.

Given the usual temperamental difficulties, the peregrinations of restless individuals, the nomadic habits of the group as a whole, and the general playfulness (their own word being the more ironic "frivolousness") of the membership, a Sewing Harem was frequently known to disband not many years after the nearly simultaneous birth of its children.

But the chief reason for the dissolution of a Sewing Harem was jealousy over the children. The children were few, the mothers many. Each child was everyone's child in the mind of the community, but by no means in the mind of the child. At first the babies were kept together in a compound, and all the mothers had equal access to them for dandling, rocking, and fondling. But of course only the mothers who could breastfeed were at all popular with the babies, since the theorists of these societies, who had a strong and authoritative caucus, frowned on bottles. Consequently, the mothers who had not experienced parturition, and who had no breast-milk, were avoided by the babies, and soon the community of mothers began to be divided into those the babies preferred and those the babies shunned; or, into milkers and non-milkers; or, into elite mothers and second-class mothers.

Somehow, even after the children were weaned, the original classifications persisted, causing depression among the second-class mothers.

As the children grew older, moreover, it was discovered that they *interrupted*. By now, several of the second-class mothers, feeling disappointed, had gone off to join other Sewing Harems just then in the process of putting themselves out for rental. And only these defeated mothers, by virtue of being no longer on the scene, were not interrupted. All the rest were. It was found that the children interrupted careers, journeys, appointments, games, telephone calls, self-development, education, meditation, sexual activity, and other enlightened, useful, and joyous pursuits. But since the children were all being brought up with the highest self-expectations, they believed themselves to be ("as indeed you are," the mothers told them) in every way central to the community.

They believed this, in spite of their understanding that, morally and philosophically, they had no right to exist. Morally: each one had been conceived by breach of contract. Philosophically: each one had been born to a mother theoretically committed to the closure of the passage leading to the womb. In brief, the children knew that they were the consequence of unpredictable deviations from a metaphysical position; or, to state it still more succinctly, the fruit of snipped stitches.

That the children interrupted the personal development of the mothers was difficulty enough. In a less dialectical community, there might have been a drive toward comfortable if imperfect solutions. But these were (as it ought by now to be radiantly clear) no ordinary women. Ordinary women might have taken turns in caring for the children, or hired men and other women for this purpose, or experimented with humane custodial alternatives. A Sewing Harem, however, was a community of philosophers. And just as bottle-feeding had been condemned as an inferior compromise, so now were the various permutations of day-care proposals scorned. Each child was regarded as the offspring not simply of a single philosopher, but of a community of philosophers; hence not to be subjected to rearing by hirelings, or by any arrangement inferior to the loftiest visions of communal good.

As for taking turns, though it might be fair, it was inconceivable: just as each child was entitled to the highest self-expectation without compromise, so was each philosopher entitled to the highest self-development without compromise or interruption.

The children as they grew not only interrupted the mothers; they interfered with the mothers' most profound ideals. The blatant fact of the birth of a large group of children hindered ecological reform, promoted pollution, and frustrated every dramatic hope of rational population reduction. In short, the presence of the children was anti-progressive. And since not only joy and self-development, but also friendship and truth, were the dearest doctrines of a Sewing Harem, the children were made to understand that, in spite of their deserving the highest self-expectations, they represented nevertheless the most regressive forces on the planet.

It is hardly necessary to note, given the short life of any novelty, that by the time the children became adults, the fad of the Sewing Harems had virtually died out (excepting, now and then, an occasional nostalgic revival). Not surprisingly, the term "Harem" itself was by now universally repudiated as regressive and repugnant, despite the spirited voluntarism and economic self-sufficiency of the original societies. But the historic influence of those early societies was felt throughout the planet.

Everywhere, including the most backward areas, women were organizing themselves for sewing, with the result, of course, that there were fewer and fewer natural mothers and more and more adoptive mothers. The elitist distinctions observed by the founding groups no longer pertained, and were, in fact, reversed by the overwhelming vote of the underdeveloped countries. Devotion to egalitarian principles put the sewn majority in the saddle; and since the majority were adoptive mothers, or women whose lives were peripheral to children, or women who had nothing to do with children at all, natural motherhood (though it continued to be practiced, with restraint, in all circles except the very literary) was little noticed and less remarked on, neither as neurosis nor as necessity. It was neither patronized nor demeaned, and it was certainly not persecuted. It was not much on anyone's mind.

It goes without saying that society at large instantly improved. The planet took on a tidier appearance: more room for gardens and trees, a diminution of garbage and poverty, fewer smoky factories, highways decently uncrowded for a holiday drive. In the international sphere, matters were somewhat less satisfactory, at least in the view of the men and women who ran the planet. Though the wicked remained dominant, as always, it was not much worthwhile making wars any more, since in any conflict it is preferable that vast and vaster quantities of lives be butchered, and the numbers of young soldiers available for losing the bottom halves of their torsos went on diminishing.

To put it as briefly and delightfully as possible: the good (those self-respecting individuals who did not intend to waste their years) had greater opportunities to add to their goodness via self-improvement and self-development, the wicked were thwarted, and the planet began to look and smell nicer than anyone had ever expected.

And all this was the legacy of a handful of Sewing Harems which had once been dismissed as a self-indulgent ideological fad.

Meanwhile, something rather sad had happened, though it applied only to a nearly imperceptible minority and seldom drew anyone's constructive attention.

The children of the Sewing Harems had become pariahs.

How this occurred is of not much interest: whether they were regarded as a laughingstock anachronism, the spawn of geishas, scions of an antiquated and surely comical social contrivance, the very reminder of which was an embarrassment to the modern temper; whether they were taken as the last shameful relic of an aggressively greedy entrepreneurial movement; whether they were scorned as personalities mercilessly repressed by the barbaric extremes of the communal impulse; whether they were damned as the offspring of the pornographic imagination; whether they were jeered at as the deformed cubs of puritanical bluestockings; whether all of these or none, no one can rightly say.

Sociologists with enough curiosity to look into the origins of the sect pointed, predictably, to their upbringing: they were taught that they were at the root of the planet's woes, and yet they were taught that they had earned not one, but many, mothers. As a consequence of the first teaching, they fulfilled themselves as irrational demons and turned themselves into outcasts. As a consequence of the second teaching, they idolized motherhood.

You will have noticed that I have referred to these unfortunates as a "sect." This is exactly true. They were content to marry only one another; or, perhaps, no one else was content to marry any of *them*. Since numbers of them had the same father, or the same natural mother, or both, they were already afflicted with the multitudinous ills of inbreeding, and their fierce adherence to endogamy compounded these misfortunes. They had harelips, limps, twisted jaws and teeth, short arms, diseases of the blood, hereditary psychoses; some were wretchedly strabismic, others blind or deaf. They were an ugly, anxious, stern-minded crew, continually reproducing themselves.

Any woman of the sect who sewed herself they would kill; but this was generally unheard of among them, since sewing was their most ferocious taboo. Male babies born in any way sexually deformed were admitted to early surgery, but female babies born with unusually small or sealed vaginas were fed cyanide. The only remaining resemblance to the gaily lucid and civilizing Sewing Harems from which these savages derived was their prohibition of bottle-feeding.

They were organized into strong family units, and emphasized family orderliness and conventionality. All this was within the tribe. Otherwise they were likely to be criminals—members of the sect were frequently convicted of having murdered sewn women. If they had any gift at all, it was for their indulgence in unusual art forms. They had a notorious talent for obscene stonecutting.

Worst of all was their religious passion. They had invented a Superior Goddess: a single unimaginative and brutish syllable of three letters, two of them identical, formed her name —ingenious nonetheless, since it was a palindrome, pronounced identically whether chanted forward or backward. The goddess was conceived as utterly carnal, with no role other than to nurture the urge to spawn; under her base auspices the tribe spewed forth dozens of newborn savages in a single day.

In addition to murdering sewn women, the descendants of the Sewing Harems were guilty of erecting religious statuary on highways in the dead of night. These appeared in the likenesses of immense round gate-pillars, which, looming without warning in the blaze of day where there had been nothing the evening before, were the cause of multiple bloody traffic accidents. The best were carved out of enormous rocks quarried no one knew where, hauled on trucks, and set in place by cranes. The cheapest were made of concrete, mixed on the spot, and left to dry behind sawhorses hung with bright rags. In police reports these structures were usually described as mammary replicas; in actuality they had the shapes of huge vulvae. Sometimes the corpse of a sewn woman, stinking of some foul incense, a shiny magazine picture of an infant nailed into her thigh, would be found between the high walls of the two horrendous labia.

I have already remarked that these primitives did not number significantly in the general population (though they were disproportionately present in the prison population). They were pests, rather than a pestilence, and their impact on the planet would without doubt have continued negligible had the imperva molecules not suddenly begun first to deteriorate in the skies, and then to disintegrate entirely. All this was inexplicable; until now every firm scientific expectation was that no such dissolution could occur except under the climatic threat of a new ice age. Such a comment was always taken for a joke. In point of fact it remained a joke. There were no extraordinary atmospheric upheavals; the normal temperature of the planet was undisturbed.

But it became of course impossible for women to sew themselves as casually, uncomplicatedly, and joyfully as they had been capable of doing for immemorial generations—ever since, in fact, that planet's version of Eden: a humane Eden, incidentally, which had passed on no unkindnesses or encumbrances, whether to women or to men.

And because of irresistible advances in technology, the vulval thread had been so improved (composed of woven particles of infertels encased in plastic, it could now withstand blood-dye) that the stitches could not be undone, except by the most difficult and dangerous surgery, which the majority eschewed, because of the side effects of reversed infertels when they are burst. The treacherous stitch-snipping of the Sewing Harems, so long a subject of mockery and infamy among those who admired both progress and honest commitment, was all at once seen to be a lost treasure of the race.

Nearly all of the sewn women remained sewn until their deaths.

And the pariahs, the only source of mothers, bred like monkeys in their triumph, until the great stone vulvae covered the planet from end to end, and the frivolous memory of the Sewing Harems was rubbed away, down to the faintest smear of legend.

[Here ends the second fragment.]

Puttermesser and Xanthippe

for Mark Podwal

I. PUTTERMESSER'S BRIEF LOVE LIFE, HER TROUBLES, HER TITLES

Puttermesser, an unmarried lawyer and civil servant of forty-six, felt attacked on all sides. The night before, her lover, Morris Rappoport, a married fund-raiser from Toronto, had walked out on her. His mysterious job included settling Soviet Jewish refugees away from the big metropolitan centers; he claimed to have fresh news of the oppressed everywhere, as well as intimate acquaintance with malcontents in numerous cities in both the Eastern and Western hemispheres. Puttermesser suspected him of instability and overdependency: a future madman. His gripe was that she read in bed too much; last night she had read aloud from Plato's *Theaetetus*:

THEODORUS: What do you mean, Socrates?
SOCRATES: The same thing as the story about the Thracian

maidservant who exercised her wit at the expense of
Thales, when he was looking up to study the stars and
tumbled down a well. She scoffed at him for being so
eager to know what was happening in the sky that he
could not see what lay at his feet. Anyone who gives his
life to philosophy is open to such mockery. It is true that
he is unaware what his next-door neighbor is doing,
hardly knows, indeed, whether the creature is a man at
all; he spends all his pains on the question, what man is,
and what powers and properties distinguish such a nature
from any other. You see what I mean, Theodorus?

Rappoport did not see. He withdrew his hand from Puttermesser's belly. "What's the big idea, Ruth?" he said.
"That's right," Puttermesser said.
"What?"
"That's just what Socrates is after: the big idea."
"You're too old for this kind of thing," Rappoport said. He
had a medium-sized, rather square, reddish mustache over
perfect teeth. His teeth were more demanding to Puttermesser's gaze than his eyes, which were so diffidently pig-
mented that they seemed whited out, like the naked eyes on a
Roman bust. His nose, however, was dominant, eloquent,
with large deep nostrils that appeared to meditate. "Cut it
out, Ruth. You're behaving like an adolescent," Rappoport
said.
"You'll never fall down a well," Puttermesser said. "You
never look up." She felt diminished; those philosophical nostrils had misled her.
"Ruth, Ruth," Rappoport pleaded, "what did I do?"
"It's what you didn't do. You didn't figure out what powers
and properties distinguish human nature from any other,"
Puttermesser said bitterly; as a feminist, she was careful never
to speak of "man's" nature. She always said "humankind"

instead of "mankind." She always wrote "he or she" instead of just "he."

Rappoport was putting on his pants. "You're too old for sex," he said meanly.

Puttermesser's reply was instantly Socratic: "Then I'm *not* behaving like an adolescent."

"If you know I have a plane to catch, how come you want to read in bed?"

"It's more comfortable than the kitchen table."

"Ruth, I came to make love to you!"

"All I wanted was to finish the *Theaetetus* first."

Now he had his coat on, and was crossing his scarf carefully at his throat, so as not to let in the cold. It was a winter night, but Puttermesser saw in this gesture that Rappoport, at the age of fifty-two, still obeyed his mother's doctrines, no matter that they were five decades old. "You wanted to finish!" he yelled. He grabbed the book from her lap. "It goes from page 847 to page 879, that's thirty-three pages—"

"I read fast," Puttermesser said.

In the morning she understood that Rappoport would never come back. His feelings were hurt. In the end he would have deserted her anyway—she had observed that, sooner or later, he told all his feelings to his wife. And not only to his wife. He was the sort of man who babbles.

The loss of Rappoport was not Puttermesser's only trouble. She had developed periodontal disease; her dentist reported— with a touch of pleasure in disaster—a sixty percent bone loss. Loss of bone, loss of Rappoport, loss of home! "Uncontrollable pockets," the dentist said. He gave her the name of a periodontist to consult. It was an emergency, he warned. Her gums were puffy, her teeth in peril of uprooting. It was as if, in the dread underworld below the visible gums, a volcano lay, watching for its moment of release. She spat blood into the sink.

The sink was a garish fake marble. Little blue fish-tiles swam around the walls. The toilet seat cover had a large blue mermaid painted on it. Puttermesser hated this bathroom. She hated her new "luxury" apartment, with its windowless slot of a kitchen and two tiny cramped rooms, the bathroom without a bathtub, the shower stall the size of a thimble, the toilet's flush handle made of light blue plastic. Her majestic apartment on the Grand Concourse in the Bronx, with its Alhambra spaciousness, had been ravaged by arsonists. Even before that, the old tenants had been dying off or moving away, one by one; junkies stole in, filling empty corridors with blood-stained newspapers, smashed bottles, dead matches in random rows like beetle tracks. On a summer evening Puttermesser arrived home from her office without possessions: her shoes were ash, her piano was ash, her piano teacher's penciled "Excellent," written in fine large letters at the top of "Humoresque" and right across the opening phrase of "Für Elise," had vanished among the cinders. Puttermesser's childhood, burned away. How prescient her mother had been to take all of Puttermesser's school compositions with her to Florida! Otherwise every evidence of Puttermesser's early mental growth might have gone under in that criminal conflagration.

The new apartment was crowded with plants: Puttermesser, who was once afflicted with what she called a "black thumb," and who had hitherto killed every green thing she put her hand to, determined now to be responsible for life. She dragged in great clay urns and sacks of vitamin-rich soil bought at Woolworth's and emptied dark earth into red pots. She seeded and conscientiously watered. Rappoport himself had lugged in, on a plastic-wheeled dolly, a tall stalk like a ladder of green bear's ears: he claimed it was an avocado tree he had grown from a pit in Toronto. It reminded Puttermesser of her mother's towering rubber plants on the Grand Concourse, in their ceiling-sweeping prime. Every window sill of Puttermesser's new apartment was fringed with fronds, foliage, soaring or drooping leaf-tips. The tough petals of blood-veined coleus strained the bedroom sunset. Puttermesser, astonished, discovered that if she remained attentive enough, she had the power to stimulate green bursts. All along the bosky walls vegetation burgeoned.

Yet Puttermesser's days were arid. Her office life was not peaceable; nothing bloomed for her. She had fallen. Out of the blue, the Mayor ousted the old Commissioner—Puttermesser's boss, the chief of the Department of Receipts and Disbursements—and replaced him with a new man, seven years younger than Puttermesser. He looked like a large-eared boy; he wore his tie pulled loose, and his neck stretched forward out of his collar; it gave him the posture of a vertical turtle. His eyes, too, were unblinkingly turtlish. It was possible, Puttermesser conceded to herself, that despite his slowly reaching neck and flattish head, the new man did not really resemble a turtle at all; it was only that his name—Alvin Turtelman—suggested the bare lidless deliberation of that immobile creature of the road. Turtelman did not preen. Puttermesser saw at once, in all that meditated motionlessness, that he was more ambitious than the last Commissioner, who had been satisfied with mere prestige, and had used his office like a silken tent decorated with viziers and hookahs. But Turtelman was patient; his steady ogle took in the whole wide trail ahead. He spoke of "restructuring," of "functioning," of "goals" and "gradations," of "levels of purpose" and "versus equations." He was infinitely abstract. "None of this is personal," he liked to say, but his voice was a surprise; it was more pliable than you would expect from the stillness of his stare. He stretched out his vowels like any New Yorker. He had brought with him a score of underlings for what he called "mapping out." They began the day late and ended early, moving from cubicle to cubicle and collecting résumés. They were all bad spellers, and their memos, alive with solecisms, made Puttermesser grieve, because they were lawyers, and Puttermesser loved the law and its language. She caressed its meticulousness. She thought of law as Apollo's chariot; she had read all the letters of Justice Oliver Wendell Holmes, Jr., to Harold Laski (three volumes) and to Sir Frederick Pollock (two). In her dream once she stood before a ship captain and became the fifth wife of Justice William O. Douglas; they honey-mooned on the pampas of Argentina. It was difficult to tell whether Turtelman's bad spellers represented the Mayor himself, or only the new Commissioner; but clearly they were scouts and spies. They reported on lateness and laxness, on backlogs and postponements, on insufficiencies and excesses, on waste and error. They issued warnings and sounded alarms; they brought pressure to bear and threatened and cautioned and gave tips. They were watchful and envious. It soon became plain that they did not understand the work.

They did not understand the work because they were, it turned out, political appointees shipped over from the Department of Hygienic Maintenance; a handful were from the Fire Department. They had already had careers as oligarchs of street-sweeping, sewers and drains, gutters, the perils of sleet, ice, rainslant, gas, vermin, fumigation, disinfection, snow removal, water supply, potholes, steam cleaning, deodorization, ventilation, abstersion, elutriation; those from the Fire Department had formerly wielded the scepter over matters of arson, hydrants, pumps, hose (measured by weight, in kilograms), incendiary bombs, rubber boots, wax polish, red paint, false alarms, sappers, marshals. They had ruled over all these corporealities, but without comprehension; they asked for frequent memos; they were "administrators." This meant they were good at arrest; not only at making arrests (the fire marshals, for instance), but at bringing everything to a stand-still, like the spindle-prick in Sleeping Beauty. In their presence the work instantly held its breath and came to a halt, as if it were a horse reined in for examination. They walked round and round the work, ruminating, speculating. They could not judge it; they did not understand it.

But they knew what it was for. It was for the spoils quota. The work, impenetrable though it was to its suzerains, proliferated with jobs; jobs blossomed with salaries; salaries were money; money was spoils. The current Mayor, Malachy ("Matt") Mavett, like all the mayors before him, was a dispenser of spoils, though publicly, of course, he declared himself morally opposed to political payoffs. He had long ago distributed the plums, the high patronage slots. All the commissioners were political friends of the Mayor. Sometimes a mayor would have more friends than there were jobs, and then this or that commissioner would suddenly be called upon to devise a whole new management level: a many-pegged perch just between the heights of direct mayoral appointment and the loftier rungs of the Civil Service. When that happened, Puttermesser would all at once discover a fresh crew of intermediate bosses appointed to loiter between herself and the Commissioner. Week after week, she would have to explain the work to them: the appointed intermediate bosses of the Department of Receipts and Disbursements did not usually know what the Department of Receipts and Disbursements *did*. By the time they found out, they vanished; they were always on the move, like minor bedouin sheikhs, to the next oasis. And when a new commissioner arrived right after an election (or, now and then, after what was officially described as "internal reorganization"—demoralization, upheaval, bloodbath), Puttermesser would once again be standing in the sanctuary of the Commissioner's deep inner office, the one with the mottled carpeting and the private toilet, earnestly explaining his rich domain to its new overlord.

Puttermesser was now an old hand, both at the work and at

the landscape of the bureaucracy. She was intimate with every folly and every fall. (Ah, but she did not expect her own fall.) She was a witness to every succession. (Ah, but she did not expect to be succeeded herself.) The bureaucracy was a faded feudal world of territory and authority and hierarchy, mainly dusty, except at those high moments of dagger and toppling. Through it all, Puttermesser was seen to be useful: this accounted for her climb. She had stuck her little finger into every cranny of every permutation of the pertinent law. Precedents sped through her brain. Her titles, movable and fictitious, traveled upward: from Assistant Corporation Counsel she became Administrative Tax Law Associate, and after that Vice Chief of Financial Affairs, and after that First Bursary Officer. All the while she felt like Alice, swallowing the potion and growing compact, nibbling the mushroom and swelling: each title was a swallow or a nibble, and not one of them signified anything but the degree of her convenience to whoever was in command. Her titles were the poetry of the bureaucracy.

The truth was that Puttermesser was now a fathomer; she had come to understand the recondite, dim, and secret journey of the City's money, the tunnels it rolled through, the transmutations, investments, multiplications, squeezings, fattenings and battenings it underwent. She knew where the money landed and where it was headed for. She knew the habits, names, and even the hot-tempered wives of three dozen bank executives on various levels. She had acquired half a dozen underlings of her own—with these she was diffident, polite; though she deemed herself a feminist, no ideology could succeed for her in aggrandizing force. Puttermesser was not aggressive. She disdained assertiveness. Her voice was like Cordelia's. At home, in bed, she went on dreaming and reading. She retained a romantic view of the British Civil Service in its heyday: the Cambridge Apostles carrying the probities of G. E. Moore to the far corners of the world, Leonard Woolf doing justice in Ceylon, the shy young Forster in India. Integrity. Uprightness. And all for the sake of imperialism, colonialism! In New York, Puttermesser had an immigrant's grandchild's dream of merit: justice, justice shalt thou pursue. Her heart beat for law, even for tax law: she saw the orderly nurturing of the democratic populace, public murals, subway windows bright as new dishes, parks with flowering borders, the bell-hung painted steeds of dizzying carousels.

Every day, inside the wide bleak corridors of the Municipal Building, Puttermesser dreamed an ideal Civil Service: devotion to polity, the citizen's sweet love of the citizenry, the light rule of reason and common sense, the City as a miniature country crowded with patriots—not fools and jingoists, but patriots true and serene; humorous affection for the idiosyncrasies of one's distinctive little homeland, each borough itself another little homeland, joy in the Bronx, elation in Queens, O happy Richmond! Children on roller skates, and over the Brooklyn Bridge the long patchwork-colored line of joggers, breathing hard above the homeland-hugging green waters.

II. PUTTERMESSER'S FALL, AND THE HISTORY OF THE GENUS GOLEM

Turtelman sent his secretary to fetch Puttermesser. It was a new secretary, a middle-aged bony acolyte, graying and testy, whom he had brought with him from the Department of Hygienic Maintenance: she had coarse eyebrows crawling upward. "This isn't exactly a good time for me to do this," Puttermesser complained. It was as if Turtelman did not trust the telephone for such a purpose. Puttermesser knew his purpose: he wanted teaching. He was puzzled, desperate. Inside his ambitiousness he was a naked boy, fearful. His office was cradled next to the threatening computer chamber; all along the walls the computer's hard flanks glittered with specks and lights. Puttermesser could hear, behind a partition, the spin of a thousand wheels, a thin threadlike murmur, as if the software men, long-haired chaps in sneakers, had set lyres out upon the great stone window sills of the Municipal Building. Walking behind the bony acolyte, Puttermesser pitied Turtelman: the Mayor had called for information—figures, indexes, collections, projections—and poor Turtelman, fresh from his half-education in the land of abstersion and elutriation, his frontal lobes still inclined toward repair of street-sweeping machinery, hung back bewildered. He had no answers for the Mayor, and no idea where the answers might be hidden; alas, the questions themselves fell on Turtelman's ears as though in a foreign tongue.

The secretary pushed open Turtelman's door, stood aside for Puttermesser, and went furiously away.

Poor Turtelman, Puttermesser thought.

Turtelman spoke: "You're out."

"Out?" Puttermesser said. It was a bitter Tuesday morning in mid-January; at that very moment, considerably south of the Municipal Building, in Washington, D.C., they were getting ready to inaugurate the next President of the United States. High politics emblazoned the day. Bureaucracies all over the world were turning on their hinges, gates were lifting and shutting, desks emptying and filling. The tide rode upon Turtelman's spittle; it glimmered on his teeth.

"As of this afternoon," Turtelman said, "you are relieved of your duties. It's nothing personal, believe me. I don't know you. We're restructuring. It's too bad you're not a bit older. You can't retire at only forty-six." He had read her résumé, then; at least that.

"I'm old enough," Puttermesser said.

"Not for collecting your pension. You people have a valuable retirement system here. I envy you. It drains the rest of us dry." The clack of his teeth showed that he was about to deliver a sting: "We ordinary folk who aren't lucky enough to be in the Civil Service can't afford you."

Puttermesser announced proudly, "I earn my way. I scored highest in the entire city on the First-Level Management Examination. I was editor-in-chief of Law Review at Yale Law School. I graduated from Barnard with honors in history, *summa cum laude*, Phi Beta Kappa—"

Turtelman broke in: "Give me two or three weeks, I'll find a little spot for you somewhere. You'll hear from me."

Thus the manner of Puttermesser's fall. Ignoble. She did not dream there was worse to come. She spilled the papers out of her drawers and carried them to a windowless cubicle down the hall from her old office. For a day or so her ex-staff averted their eyes; then they ceased to notice her; her replacement had arrived. He was Adam Marmel, late of the Bureau of Emergencies, an old classmate of Turtelman's at New York University, where both had majored in Film Arts. This interested Puttermesser: the Department of Receipts and Disbursements was now in the hands of young men who had been trained to pursue illusion, to fly with a gossamer net after fleeting shadows. They were attracted to the dark, where fraudulent emotions raged. They were, moreover, close friends, often together. The Mayor had appointed Turtelman; Turtelman had appointed Marmel; Marmel had succeeded Puttermesser, who now sat with the *Times*, deprived of light, isolated, stripped, forgotten. An outcast. On the next Friday her salary check came as usual. But no one called her out of her cubicle.

Right in the middle of business hours—she no longer had

any business, she was perfectly idle—Puttermesser wrote a letter to the Mayor:

The Honorable Malachy Mavett
Mayor, City of New York
City Hall

Dear Mayor Mavett:
Your new appointee in the Department of Receipts and ·Disbursements, Commissioner Alvin Turtelman, has forced a fine civil servant of honorable temperament, with experience both wide and impassioned, out of her job. I am that civil servant. Without a hearing, without due process, without a hope of appeal or redress (except, Mr. Mayor, by you!), Commissioner Turtelman has destroyed a career in full flower. Employing an affectless vocabulary by means of which, in a single instant, he abruptly ousted a civil servant of high standing, Commissioner Turtelman has politicized a job long held immune to outside preferment. In a single instant, honor, dignity, and continuity have been snatched away! I have been professionally injured and personally humiliated. I have been rendered useless. As of this writing I am costing the City's taxpayers the price of my entire salary, while I sit here working a crossword puzzle; while I hold this very pen. No one looks at me. They are embarrassed and ashamed. At first a few ex-colleagues came into this little abandoned office (where I do nothing) to offer condolences, but that was only at first. It is like being at my own funeral, Mr. Mayor, only imagine it!
Mr. Mayor, I wish to submit several urgent questions to you; I will be grateful for your prompt views on these matters of political friendships, connections, and power.
1. Are you aware of this inequitable treatment of

professional staff in the Bureau of Summary Sessions of the Department of Receipts and Disbursements?

2. If so, is this the nature of the Administration you are content to be represented by?

3. Is it truly your desire to erode and undermine the professional Civil Service—one of democratic government's most just, most equitable, devices?

4. Does Commissioner Alvin Turtelman's peremptory action really reflect your own sensibility, with all its fairness and exuberant humaneness?

In City, State, and World life, Mr. Mayor (I have observed this over many years), power and connections are never called power and connections. They are called principle. They are called democracy. They are called judgment. They are called doing good. They are called restructuring. They are called exigency. They are called improvement. They are called functioning. They are called the common need. They are called government. They are called running the Bureau, the Department, the City, the State, the World, looking out for the interests of the people.

Mr. Mayor, getting the spoils is called anything but getting the spoils!

Puttermesser did not know whether Malachy ("Matt") Mavett's sensibility was really fair and exuberantly humane; she had only put that in to flatter him. She had glimpsed the Mayor in the flesh only once or twice, at a meeting, from a distance. She had also seen him on Sunday morning television, at a press conference, but then he was exceptionally cautious and sober; before the cameras he was neuter, he had no sensibility at all; he was nearly translucent. His white mustache looked tangled; his white hair twirled in strings over his temples.

Puttermesser's letter struck her as gripping, impressive; copying it over on the typewriter at home that night, she felt how the Mayor would be stabbed through by such fevered eloquence. How remorseful he would be, how moved!

Still another salary check arrived. It was not for the usual amount; Puttermesser's pay had been cut. The bony acolyte appeared with a memo from Turtelman: Puttermesser was to leave her barren cubicle and go to an office with a view of the Woolworth Building, and there she was to take up the sad life of her demotion.

Turtelman had shoved her into the lowliest ranks of Taxation. It was an unlikely post for a mind superfctate with Idea; Puttermesser felt the malignancy behind this shift. Her successor had wished her out of sight. "I do not consort with failure," she heard Adam Marmel tell one of the auditors. She lived now surrounded by auditors—literal-minded men. They read best-sellers; their fingers were smudged from the morning papers, which they clutched in their car pools or on the subway from Queens. One of them, Leon Cracow, a bachelor from Forest Hills who wore bow ties and saddle shoes, was engaged in a tedious litigation: he had once read a novel and fancied himself its hero. The protagonist wore bow ties and saddle shoes. Cracow was suing for defamation. "My whole love life's maligned in there," he complained to Puttermesser. He kept the novel on his desk—it was an obscure book no one had ever heard of, published by a shadowy California press. Cracow had bought it remaindered for eighty-nine cents and ruminated over it every day. Turning the pages, he wet two of his fingers repeatedly. The novel was called *Pyke's Pique*; a tax auditor named John McCracken Pyke was its chief character. "McCracken," Cracow said, "that's practically Cracow. It sounds practically identical. Listen, in the book this guy goes to prostitutes. I don't go to prostitutes! The skunk's got me all wrong. He's destroying my good name." Sometimes Cracow asked Puttermesser for her opinion of his lawyer's last move. Puttermesser urged him on. She believed in the uses of fantasy. "A person should see himself or herself everywhere," she said. "All things manifest us."

The secret source of this motto was, in fact, her old building on the Grand Concourse. Incised in a stone arch over the broad front door, and also in Puttermesser's loyal brain, were these Roman-style tracings: LONGWOOD ARMS, No. 26. GREENDALE HALL, No. 28. ALL THINGS MANIFEST US. The builder had thought deep thoughts, and Cracow was satisfied. "Ruth," he said, "you take the cake." As usual, he attempted to date her. "Any concert, any show, you name it," he said; "I'm a film buff." "You fit right in with Turtelman and Marmel," Puttermesser said. "Not me," Cracow retorted, "with me it's nostalgia only. My favorite movie is Deanna Durbin, Leopold Stokowski, and Adolphe Menjou in *One Hundred Men and a Girl*. Wholesome, sweet, not like they make today. Light classical. Come on, Ruth, it's at the Museum of Modern Art, in the cellar." Puttermesser turned him down. She knew she would never marry, but she was not yet reconciled to childlessness. Sometimes the thought that she would never give birth tore her heart.

She imagined daughters. It was self-love: all these daughters were Puttermesser as a child. She imagined a daughter in fourth grade, then in seventh grade, then in second-year high school. Puttermesser herself had gone to Hunter College High School and studied Latin. At Barnard she had not renounced Catullus and Vergil. *O infelix Dido*, chanted the imaginary daughter, doing her Latin homework at Puttermesser's new Danish desk in the dark corner of the little bedroom. It was a teak rectangle; Puttermesser still had not bought a lamp for it. She hated it that all her furniture was new.

No reply came from the Mayor: not even a postcard of acknowledgment from an underling. Malachy ("Matt") Mavett was ignoring Puttermesser.

Rappoport had abandoned the Sunday *Times*, purchased

Saturday night at the airport; he had left it, unopened, on the Danish desk. Puttermesser swung barefoot out of bed, stepped over Plato, and reached for Rappoport's *Times*. She brooded over his furry chest hair, yellowing from red. Now the daughter, still in high school, was memorizing Goethe's *Erlkönig:*

> *Dem Vater grauset's, er reitet geschwind,*
> *Er hält in Armen des ächzende Kind,*
> *Erreicht den Hof mit Mühe und Not:*
> *In seinem Armen das Kind war tot.*

The words made Puttermesser want to sob. The child was dead. In its father's arms the child was dead. She came back to bed, carrying Rappoport's *Times*. It was as heavy as if she carried a dead child. The Magazine Section alone was of a preternatural weight. Advertising. Consumerism. Capitalism. Page after page of cars, delicately imprinted chocolates, necklaces, golden whiskey. Affluence while the poor lurked and mugged, hid in elevators, shot drugs into their veins, stuck guns into old grandmothers' tremulous and brittle spines, in covert pools of blackness released the springs of their bright-flanked switchblades, in shafts, in alleys, behind walls, in ditches.

A naked girl lay in Puttermesser's bed. She looked dead— she was all white, bloodless. It was as if she had just undergone an epileptic fit: her tongue hung out of her mouth. Her eyelids were rigidly ajar; they had no lashes, and the skin was so taut and thin that the eyeballs bulged through. Her palms had fallen open; they were a clear white. Her arms were cold rods. A small white square was visible on the tongue. The girl did not resemble Puttermesser at all; she was certainly not one of the imaginary daughters. Puttermesser moved to one side of the bed, then circled back around the foot to the other side. She put on her slippers; summoning reason, she continued to move around and around the bed. There was no doubt that a real body was in it. Puttermesser reached out and touched the right shoulder—a reddish powder coated her fingers. The body seemed filmed with sand, or earth, or grit; some kind of light clay. Filth. A filthy junkie or prostitute; both. Sickness and filth. Rappoport, stalking away in the middle of the night, had been careless about closing the apartment door. God only knew where the creature had concealed herself, what had been stolen or damaged. When Puttermesser's back was turned, the filthy thing had slid into her bed. Such a civilized bed, the home of Plato and other high-minded readings. The body had a look of perpetuity about it, as if it had always been reclining there, in Puttermesser's own bed; yet it was a child's body, the limbs stretched into laxity and languor. She was a little thing, no more than fifteen: Puttermesser saw how the pubic hair was curiously sparse; but the breasts were nearly not there at all. Puttermesser went on calculating and circling: should she call the super, or else telephone for an ambulance? New York! What was the good of living in a tiny squat box, with low ceilings, on East Seventy-first Street, a grudging landlord, a doorman in an admiral's uniform, if there were infiltrators, addicts, invaders, just the same as on the fallen Grand Concourse?

Puttermesser peered down at the creature's face. Ugly. The nose and mouth were clumsily formed, as if by some coarse hand that had given them a negligent tweak. The vomerine divider was off-center, the nostrils unpleasantly far apart. The mouth was in even worse condition—also off-center, but somehow more carelessly made, with lips that failed to match, the lower one no better than a line, the upper one amazingly fat, swollen, and the narrow tongue protruding with its white patch. Puttermesser reached out a correcting hand, and then withdrew it. Once again the dust left deep red ovals on her fingertips. But it was clear that the nostrils needed pinching to bring them closer together, so Puttermesser tentatively pinched. The improvement was impressive. She blew into the left nostril to get rid of a tuft of dust; it solidified and rolled out like a clay bead. With squeamish deliberation she pushed the nose in line with the middle space where the eyebrows ought to have been. There were no eyebrows, no eyelashes, no fingernails, no toenails. The thing was defective, unfinished. The mouth above all required finishing. Forming and re-forming the savage upper lip, getting into the mood of it now, Puttermesser wished she were an artist or sculptor: she centered the mouth, thickened the lower lip with a quick turn, smoothed out the hunch of the upper one—the tongue was in the way. She peeled off the white square and, pressing hard, shoved the tongue back down into the mouth.

The bit of white lay glimmering in Puttermesser's palm. It seemed to be nothing more than an ordinary slip of paper, but she thought she ought to put it aside to look it over more carefully after a while, so she left the bed and set it down on the corner of the teak desk. Then she came back and glanced up and down the body, to see whether there was anything else that called for correction. A forefinger needed lengthening, so Puttermesser tugged at it. It slid as if boneless, like taffy, cold but not sticky, and thrillingly pliable. Still, without its nail a finger can shock; Puttermesser recoiled. Though the face was now normal enough, there was more to be done. Something had flashed upward from that tongue-paper—the white patch was blank; yet it was not only blank. Puttermesser carried it in her palm to the window, for the sake of the light. But on the sill and under the sill every pot was cracked, every green plant sprawled. The roots, skeletal and hairy, had been torn from their embracing soil—or, rather, the earth had been scooped away. The plain earth, stolen. Puttermesser, holding the white scrap, wandered from window to window. There was no pot that had not been vandalized in the same way—Rappoport's big clay urn was in shards, the avocado tree broken. A few sparse grains of soil powdered the floor. Not a plant anywhere had been left unmolested—all the earth in Puttermesser's apartment was gone; taken away; robbed.

In the bedroom the girl's form continued its lethal sleep. Puttermesser lifted the tiny paper to the bright panes. Out of the whiteness of the white patch another whiteness flickered, as though a second version of absence were struggling to swim up out of the aboriginal absence. For Puttermesser, it was as if the white of her own eye could suddenly see what the purposeful retina had shunned. It was in fact not so much a seeing as the sharpness of a reading, and what Puttermesser read—she whose intellectual passions were pledged to every alphabet—was a single primeval Hebrew word, shimmering with its lightning holiness, the Name of Names, that which one dare not take in vain. Aloud she uttered it:

חשם,

whereupon the inert creature, as if drilled through by electricity, as if struck by some principle of instantaneous vitality, leaped straight from the bed; Puttermesser watched the fingernails grow rapidly into place, and the toenails, and the eyebrows and lashes: complete. A configuration of freckles appeared on the forehead. The hair of the head and of the mons Veneris thickened, curled, glistened dark red, the color of clay; the creature had risen to walk. She did it badly, knocking down the desk-chair and bumping into the dresser. Sick, drugged, drunk; vandal; thief of earth!

"Get your clothes on and get out," Puttermesser said. Where were the thing's clothes? She had none; she seemed less pale moment by moment; she was lurching about in her skin. She was becoming rosy. A lively color was in her cheeks and hands. The mouth, Puttermesser's own handiwork, was vivid. Puttermesser ran to her closet and pulled out a shirt, a skirt, a belt, a cardigan. From her drawers she swept up bra, pantyhose, slip. There was only the question of shoes. "Here," she said, "summer sandals, that's all I can spare. Open toes, open heels, they'll fit. Get dressed. I can give you an old coat—go ahead. Sit down on the bed. Put this stuff on. You're lucky I'm not calling the police."

The creature staggered away from the bed, toward the teak desk.

"Do what I say!"

The creature had seized a notepad and a ballpoint pen, and was scribbling with shocking speed. Her fingers, even the newly lengthened one, were rhythmically coordinated. She clenched the pen, Puttermesser saw, like an experienced writer: as if the pen itself were a lick of the tongue, or an extension of the thinking digits. It surprised Puttermesser to learn that this thief of earth was literate. In what language? And would she then again try to swallow what she wrote, leaving one untouchable word behind?

The thing ripped away the alphabet-speckled page, tottered back with the pad, and laid the free sheet on the pillow.

"What's the matter? Can't you walk?" Puttermesser asked; she thought of afflicted children she had known, struck by melancholy witherings and dodderings.

But the answer was already on the paper. Puttermesser read: "I have not yet been long up upon my fresh-made limbs. Soon my gait will come to me. Consider the newborn colt. I am like unto that. All tongues are mine, especially that of my mother. Only speech is forbidden me."

A lunatic! Cracked! Alone in the house with a maniac; a deaf-mute to boot. "Get dressed," Puttermesser again commanded.

The thing wrote: "I hear and obey the one who made me."

"What the hell *is* this," Puttermesser said flatly.

The thing wrote: "My mother," and rapidly began to jerk herself into Puttermesser's clothes, but with uneven sequences of the body—the more vitality the creature gained, the more thinglike she seemed.

Puttermesser was impatient; she longed to drive the creature out. "Put on those shoes," she ordered.

The thing wrote: "No."

"Shoes!" Puttermesser shouted. She made a signpost fist and flung it in the direction of the door. "Go out the way you came in!"

The thing wrote: "No shoes. This is a holy place. I did not enter. I was formed. Here you spoke the Name of the Giver of Life. You blew in my nostril and encouraged my soul. You circled my clay seven times. You enveloped me with your spirit. You pronounced the Name and brought me to myself. Therefore I call you mother."

Puttermesser's lungs began to roil. It was true she had circled the creature on the bed. Was it seven times around? It was true she had blown some foreign matter out of the nose. Had she blown some uncanny energy into an entrance of the dormant body? It was true she had said aloud one of the Names of the Creator.

The thing wrote again: "Mother. Mother."

"Go away!"

The thing wrote: "You made me."

"I didn't give birth to you." She would never give birth. Yet she had formed this mouth—the creature's mute mouth. She looked at the mouth: she saw what she had made.

The thing wrote: "Earth is my flesh. For the sake of my flesh you carried earth to this high place. What will you call me?"

A new turbulence fell over Puttermesser. She had always imagined a daughter named Leah. "Leah," she said.

"No," the creature wrote. "Leah is my name, but I want to be Xanthippe."

Puttermesser said, "Xanthippe was a shrew. Xanthippe was Socrates' wife."

"I want to be Xanthippe," the thing wrote. "I know everything you know. I am made of earth but also I am made out of your mind. Now watch me walk."

The thing walked, firmly, with a solid thump of a step and no stumbling. She wrote on the pad: "I am becoming stronger. You made me. I will be of use to you. Don't send me away. Call me what I prefer, Xanthippe."

"Xanthippe," Puttermesser said.

She succumbed; her throat panted. It came to her that the creature was certainly not lying: Puttermesser's fingernails were crowded with grains of earth. In some unknown hour after Rappoport's departure in the night, Puttermesser had shaped an apparition. She had awakened it to life in the conventional way. Xanthippe was a golem, and what had polymathic Puttermesser *not* read about the genus golem?

Puttermesser ordered: "All right, go look on the bookshelves. Bring me whatever you see on your own kind."

The creature churned into the living room and hurried back with two volumes, one in either hand; she held the pen ready in her mouth. She dumped the books on the bed and wrote: "I am the first female golem."

"No you're not," Puttermesser said. It was clear that the creature required correction. Puttermesser flew through the pages of one of the books. "Ibn Gabirol created a woman. This was in Spain, long ago, the eleventh century. The king gave him a dressing-down for necromancy, so he dismantled her. She was made of wood and had hinges—it was easy to take her apart."

The creature wrote: "That was not a true golem."

"Go sit down in a corner," Puttermesser said. "I want to read."

The creature obeyed. Puttermesser dived into the two volumes. She had read them many times before; she knew certain passages nearly verbatim. One, a strange old text in a curiously awkward English translation (it was printed in Austria in 1925), had the grass-green public binding of a library book; to Puttermesser's citizenly shame, she had never returned it. It had been borrowed from the Crotona Park Branch decades ago, in Puttermesser's adolescence. There were photographs in it, incandescently clear: of graves, of a statue, of the lamp-hung interior of a synagogue in Prague—the Altneuschul—, of its tall peaked contour, of the two great clocks, one below the cupola, the other above it, on the venerable Prague Jewish Community House. Across the street from the Community House there was a shop, with a sign that said v. PRESSLER in large letters; underneath, his hand in his pocket, a dapper mustached dandy in a black fedora lounged eternally. Familiar, static, piercingly distinct though these illustrations were, Puttermesser all the same felt their weary old ache: phantoms—v. PRESSLER a speck of earth; the houses air; the dandy evaporated. Among these aged streets and deranged structures Puttermesser's marveling heart had often prowled. "You have no feelings," Rappoport once told her: he meant that she had the habit of flushing with ideas as if they were passions.

And this was true. Puttermesser's intelligence, brambly with the confusion of too much history, was a private warted tract, rubbled over with primordial statuary. She was painfully anthropological. Civilizations rolled into her rib cage, stone after graven stone: cuneiform, rune, cipher. She had pruned out allegory, metaphor; Puttermesser was no mystic, enthusiast, pneumaticist, ecstatic, kabbalist. Her mind was clean; she was a rationalist. Despite the imaginary daughters—she included these among her losses—she was not at all attached to any notion of shade or specter, however corporeal it might appear, and least of all to the idea of a golem—

hardly that, especially now that she had the actual thing on her hands. What transfixed her was the kind of intellect (immensely sober, pragmatic, unfanciful, rationalist like her own) to which a golem ordinarily occurred—occurred, that is, in the shock of its true flesh and absolute being. The classical case of the golem of Prague, for instance: the Great Rabbi Judah Loew, circa 1520–1609, maker of that renowned local creature, was scarcely one of those misty souls given over to untrammeled figments or romances. He was, instead, a reasonable man of biting understanding, a solid scholar, a pragmatic leader—a learned quasi-mayor. What he understood was that the scurrilous politics of his city, always tinged with religious interests, had gone too far. In short, they were killing the Jews of Prague. It had become unsafe for a peddler to open his pack, or a merchant his shop; no mother and her little daughter dared turn into an alley. Real blood ran in the streets, and all on account of a rumor of blood: citizens of every class—not just the guttersnipes—were muttering that the Jews had kneaded the bodies of Christian infants into their sacral Passover wafers. Scapegoat Jews, exposed, vulnerable, friendless, unarmed! The very Jews forbidden by their dietary code to eat an ordinary farmyard egg tainted with the minutest jot of fetal blood! So the Great Rabbi Judah Loew, to defend the Jews of Prague against their depredators, undertook to fashion a golem.

Puttermesser was well acquainted with the Great Rabbi Judah Loew's method of golem-making. It was classical; it was, as such things go, ordinary. To begin with, he entered a dream of Heaven, wherein he asked the angels to advise him. The answer came in alphabetical order: *afar, esh, mayim, ruach*: earth, fire, water, wraith. With his son-in-law, Isaac ben Shimshon, and his pupil, Jacob ben Chayim Sasson, the Great Rabbi Judah Loew sought inner purity and sanctification by means of prayer and ritual immersion; then the three of them went out to a mud-bed on the banks of the River Moldau to create a man of clay. Three went out; four returned. They worked by torchlight, reciting Psalms all the while, molding a human figure. Isaac ben Shimshon, a descendant of the priests of the Temple, walked seven times around the clay heap bulging up from the ground. Jacob ben Chayim Sasson, a Levite, walked seven times around. Then the Great Rabbi Judah Loew himself walked around, once only, and placed a parchment inscribed with the Name into the clay man's mouth. The priest represented fire; the Levite water; the Great Rabbi Judah Loew designated himself spirit and wraith, or air itself. The earth-man lay inert upon earth, like upon like. Fire, water, air, all chanted together: "And he breathed into his nostrils the breath of life; and man became a living soul"—whereupon the golem heated up, turned fiery red, and rose! It rose to become the savior of the Jews of Prague. On its forehead were imprinted the three letters that are the Hebrew word for truth: *aleph, mem, tav.*

This history Puttermesser knew, in its several versions, inside out. "Three went out; four returned"—following which, how the golem punished the slaughterers, persecutors, predators! How it cleansed Prague of evil and infamy, of degeneracy and murder, of vice and perfidy! But when at last the Great Rabbi Judah Loew wished the golem to subside, he climbed a ladder (a golem grows bigger every day), reached up to the golem's forehead, and erased the letter *aleph.* Instantly the golem fell lifeless, given back to spiritless clay: lacking the *aleph,* the remaining letters, *mem* and *tav,* spelled *met*—dead. The golem's body was hauled up to the attic of the Altneuschul, where it still rests among ever-thickening cobwebs. "No one may touch the cobwebs," ran one of the stories, "for whoever touches them dies."

For Puttermesser, the wonder of this tale was not in any of its remarkable parts, familiar as they were, and not even in its recurrence. The golem recurred, of course. It moved from the Exile of Babylon to the Exile of Europe; it followed the Jews. In the third century Rabbi Rava created a golem, and sent it to Rabbi Zera, who seemed not to know it was a golem until he discovered that it could not speak. Then realization of the thing's true nature came to him, and he rebuked it: "You must have been made by my comrades of the Talmudic Academy; return to your dust." Rabbi Hanina and Rabbi Oshaya were less successful than Rabbi Rava; they were only able to produce a very small calf, on which they dined. An old kabbalistic volume, the Book of Creation, explains that Father Abraham himself could manufacture human organisms. The Book of Raziel contains a famous workable prescription for golem-making: the maker utilizes certain chants and recitations, imprinted medals, esoteric names, efficacious shapes and totems. Ben Sira and his father, the prophet Jeremiah, created a golem, in the logical belief that Adam himself was a golem; their golem, like Adam, had the power of speech. King Nebuchadnezzar's own idol turned into a living golem when he set on its head the diadem of the High Priest, looted out of the Temple in Jerusalem; the jeweled letters of the Tetragrammaton were fastened into the diadem's silver sockets. The prophet Daniel, pretending to kiss the king's golem, swiftly plucked out the gems that spelled the Name of God, and the idol was again lifeless. Even before that, thieves among the wicked generation that built the Tower of Babel swiped some of the contractor's materials to fashion idols, which were made to walk by having the Name shoved into their mouths; then they were taken for gods. Rabbi Aharon of Baghdad and Rabbi Hananel did not mold images; instead, they sewed parchments inscribed with the Name into the right arms of corpses, who at once revived and became members of the genus golem. The prophet Micah made a golden calf that could dance, and Bezalel, the designer of the Tabernacle, knew how to combine letters of the alphabet so as to duplicate Creation, both heaven and earth. Rabbi Elazar of Worms had a somewhat similar system for golem-making: three adepts must gather up "virginal mountain earth," pour running water over it, knead it into a man, bury it, and recite two hundred and twenty-one alphabetical combinations, observing meticulously the prescribed order of the vowels and consonants. But Abraham Abulafia could make a man out of a mere spoonful of earth by blowing it over an ordinary dish of water; undoubtedly this had some influence on Paracelsus, the sixteenth-century German alchemist, who used a retort to make a homunculus: Paracelsus's manikin, however, was not telluric, being composed of blood, sperm, and urine, from which the Jewish golem-makers recoiled. For the Jews, earth, water, and the divine afflatus were the only permissible elements—the afflatus being summoned through the holy syllables. Rabbi Ishmael, on the other hand, knew another way of withdrawing that life-conferring holiness and rendering an active golem back into dust: he would recite the powerful combinations of sacred letters backward, meanwhile circling the creature in the direction opposite to the one that had quickened it.

There was no end to the conditions of golem-making, just as there was no end to the appearance of one golem after another in the pullulating procession of golem-history; but Puttermesser's brain, crowded with all these acquisitions and rather a tidy store of others (for instance, she had the noble Dr. Gershom Scholem's bountiful essay "The Idea of the Golem" virtually by heart), was unattracted either to number or to method. What interested Puttermesser was something else: it was the plain fact that the golem-makers were neither visionaries nor magicians nor sorcerers. They were neither fantasists nor fabulists nor poets. They were, by and large, scientific realists—and, in nearly every case at hand, serious scholars and intellectuals: the plausible forerunners, in fact, of their great-grandchildren, who are physicists, biologists, or logical positivists. It was not only the Great Rabbi Judah Loew, the esteemed golem-maker of Prague, who had, in addition, a reputation as a distinguished Talmudist, reasoner, philosopher; even Rabbi Elijah, the most celebrated Jewish intellect of Eastern Europe (if Spinoza is the most celebrated on the Western side), whose brilliance outstripped the fame of every other scholar, who founded the most rigorous rabbinical academy in the history of the cold lands, who at length became known as the Vilna *Gaon* (the Genius of the city of Vilna, called, on his account, the Jerusalem of the North)— even the Vilna *Gaon* once attempted, before the age of thirteen, to make a golem! And the Vilna *Gaon*, with his stern refinements of exegesis and analysis, with his darting dazzlements of logical penetration, was—as everyone knows—the scourge of mystics, protester (*mitnagid*) against the dancing hasidim, scorner of those less limber minds to the Polish south, in superstitiously pious Galicia. If the Vilna *Gaon* could contemplate the making of a golem, thought Puttermesser, there was nothing irrational in it, and she would not be ashamed of what she herself had concocted.

She asked Xanthippe: "Do you eat?"

The golem wrote, "*Vivo, ergo edo.* I live, therefore I eat."

"Don't pull that on me—my Latin is as good as yours. Can you cook?"

"I can do what I must, if my mother decrees it," the golem wrote.

"All right," Puttermesser said. "In that case you can stay. You can stay until I decide to get rid of you. Now make lunch. Cook something I like, only better than I could do it."

III. THE GOLEM COOKS, CLEANS, AND SHOPS

The golem hurried off to the kitchen. Puttermesser heard the smack of the refrigerator, the clatter of silver, the faucet turned on and off; sounds of chopping in a wooden bowl; plates set out, along with an eloquent tinkle of glassware; a distant whipping, a distant sizzling; mushroom fragrances; coffee. The golem appeared at the bedroom door with a smug sniff, holding out her writing pad:

"I can have uses far beyond the mere domestic."

"If you think you're too good for kitchen work," Puttermesser retorted, "don't call yourself Xanthippe. You're so hot on aspiration, you might as well go the whole hog and pick Socrates."

The golem wrote: "I mean to be a critic, even of the highest philosophers. Xanthippe alone had the courage to gainsay Socrates. Nay, I remain Xanthippe. Please do not allow my Swedish mushroom soufflé to sink. It is best eaten in a steaming condition."

Puttermesser muttered, "I don't like your prose style. You write like a translation from the Middle Finnish. Improve it," but she followed the golem into the little kitchen. The golem's step was now light and quick, and the kitchen too seemed transformed—a floating corner of buoyancy and quicksilver: it was as if the table were in the middle of a Parisian concourse, streaming, gleaming: it had the look of a painting, both transient and eternal, a place where you sat for a minute to gossip, and also a place where the middle-aged Henry James came every day so that nothing in the large world would be lost on him. "You've set things up nicely enough,"

Puttermesser said; "I forgot all about these linen placemats." They were, in fact, part of her "trousseau"; her mother had given her things. It was expected, long ago, that Puttermesser would marry.

The golem's soufflé was excellent; she had also prepared a dessert that was part mousse, part lemon gelatin. Puttermesser, despite her periodontic troubles, took a greedy second helping. The golem's dessert was more seductive even than fudge; and fudge for Puttermesser was notoriously paradisal.

"First-rate," Puttermesser said; the golem had been standing all the while. "Aren't you having any?"

Immediately the golem sat down and ate.

"Now I'm going for a walk," Puttermesser announced. "Clean all this up. Make the bed. Be sure to mop under it. Look in the hamper, you'll find a heap of dirty clothes. There's a public washing machine in the basement. I'll give you quarters."

The golem turned glum.

"Well, look," Puttermesser argued, "I can use you for anything I please, right?"

The golem wrote, "The Great Rabbi Judah Loew's wife sent the golem of Prague to fetch water, and he fetched, and he fetched, until he flooded the house, the yard, the city, and finally the world."

"Don't bother me with fairy tales," Puttermesser said.

The golem wrote, "I insist I am superior to mere household use."

"No one's superior to dirty laundry," Puttermesser threw back, and went out into the great city. She intended to walk and brood; though she understood at last how it was that she had brought the golem to life, it disturbed her that she did not recall *making* her—emptying all the plant pots, for instance. Nor was Puttermesser wise to her own secret dictates in creating the golem. And now that the golem was actually in the house, what was to be done with her? Puttermesser worried about the landlord, a suspicious fellow. The landlord allowed no dogs or—so the lease read—"irregular relationships." She thought of passing Xanthippe off as an adopted daughter —occasionally she would happen on an article about single parents of teen-age foster children. It was not so unusual. But even that would bring its difficulty, because—to satisfy the doorman and the neighbors—such a child would have to be sent to school; and it was hardly reasonable, Puttermesser saw, to send the golem to an ordinary high school. They would ship her off to an institution for deaf-mutes, to learn sign language—and it would become evident soon enough, wouldn't it, that the golem was not the least bit deaf? There was really no place for her in any classroom; she probably knew too much already. The erratic tone of her writing, with its awful pastiche, suggested that she had read ten times more than any other tenth-grader of the same age. Besides, did the golem *have* an age? She had the shape of a certain age, yes; but the truth was she was only a few hours old. Her public behavior was bound to be unpredictable.

Puttermesser was walking northward. Her long introspective stride had taken her as far as Eighty-sixth Street. She left Madison and veered up Lexington. She had forgotten her gloves; her fingers were frozen. February's flying newspapers scuttled over broken bottles and yogurt cups squashed in the gutter. A bag lady slept in a blue-black doorway, wrapped in a pile of ragged coats. Dusk was coming down; all the store windows, without exception, were barred or shuttered against the late-afternoon Sunday emptiness. Burglars, addicts, marauders, the diverse criminal pestilences of uptown and downtown, would have to find other ways of entry: breaking through a roof; a blowtorch on a steel bar; a back toilet window with a loose grill. Ingenuity. Puttermesser peered around behind her for the mugger who, in all logic, should have been stalking her; no one was there. But she was ready: she had left her wallet at home on purpose; a police whistle dangled on a cord around her neck; she fondled the little knife in her pocket. New York! All the prisons in the metropolitan area were reputed to be hopelessly overcrowded.

At Ninety-second Street she swung through the revolving doors of the Y to warm up. The lobby was mostly uninhabited; a short line straggled toward the ticket office. Puttermesser read the poster: a piano concert at eight o'clock. She headed downtown. It was fully dark now. She reflected that it would be easy enough to undo, to reverse, the golem; there was really no point in keeping her on. For one thing, how would the golem be occupied all day while Puttermesser was at work? And Puttermesser was nervous: she had her demotion to think about. Stripped. Demoralized. That pest Cracow. Turtelman and Marmel. The Civil Service, founded to eradicate patronage, nepotism, favoritism, spoils, payoffs, injustice, corruption! Lost, all lost. The Mayor had no intention of answering Puttermesser's urgent letter.

Taking off her coat, Puttermesser called to the golem, "What's going on in there?" An unexpected brilliance spilled out of the bedroom: a lamp in the form of the Statue of Liberty stood on the teak desk. "What's this?"

"I bought it," the golem wrote. "I did everything my mother instructed. I cleaned up the kitchen, made the bed"—a new blue bedspread, with pictures of baseball mitts, covered it—"mopped the whole house, did the laundry, ironed everything, hung my mother's blouses and put my mother's pantyhose into the drawer—"

Puttermesser grabbed the sheet of paper right off the golem's pad and tore it up without reading the rest of it. "What do you mean you bought it? What kind of junk is this? I don't want the Statue of Liberty! I don't want baseball mitts!"

"It was all I could find," the golem wrote on a fresh page. "All the stores around here are closed on Sunday. I had to go down to Delancey Street on the Lower East Side. I took a taxi."

"Taxi! You'll shop when I tell you to shop!" Puttermesser yelled. "Otherwise you stay home!"

"I need a wider world," the golem wrote. "Take me with you to your place of employment tomorrow."

"My foot I will," Puttermesser said. "I've had enough of you. I've been thinking"—she looked for a euphemism— "about sending you back."

"Back?" the golem wrote; her mouth had opened all the way.

"You've got a crooked tooth. Come here," Puttermesser said, "I'll fix it."

The golem wrote, "You can no longer alter my being or any part of my being. The speaking of the Name fulfills; it precludes alteration. But I am pleasant to look on, am I not? I will not again gape so that my crooked tooth can offend my mother's eye. Only use me."

"You've got rotten taste."

The golem wrote, "It was my task to choose between baseball mitts and small raccoons intermingled with blue-eyed panda bears. The baseball mitts struck me as the lesser evil."

"I never *wanted* a bedspread," Puttermesser objected. "When I said to make the bed I just meant to straighten the blankets, that's all. And my God, the Statue of Liberty!"

The golem wrote, "A three-way bulb, 150 watts. I thought it so very clever that the bulb goes right into the torch."

"Kitsch. And where'd you get the money?"

"Out of your wallet. But see how pleasantly bright," the golem wrote. "I fear the dark. The dark is where pre-existence abides. It is not possible to think of pre-existence, but one dreads its facsimile: post-existence. Do not erase, obliterate, or annihilate me. Mother, my mother. I will serve you. Use me in the wide world."

"You stole my money right out of my wallet, spent a fortune on a taxi, and brought home the cheapest sort of junk. If you pull this kind of thing in the house, don't talk to me about the wide world!"

IV. XANTHIPPE AT WORK

But the next morning the golem was in Puttermesser's office.

"Who's the kid?" Cracow asked.

"Marmel's letting me have a typist," Puttermesser said.

"Marmel? That don't make sense. After demoting you?"

"I was reassigned," Puttermesser said; but her cheeks stung.

"Them's the breaks," Cracow said. "So how come the royal treatment? You could use the typing pool like the rest of us."

"Turtelman's put me on a special project."

"Turtelman? Turtelman kicked you in the head. What special project?"

"I'm supposed to check out any employee who broods about lawsuits on City time," Puttermesser said.

"Oh come on, Ruth, can the corn. You know damn well I've been maligned. My lawyer says I have a case. I damn well have a case. What's the kid's name?"

"Leah."

"Leah." Cracow pushed his face right into the golem's. "Do they hire 'em that young? What are you, Leah, a high-school dropout?"

"She's smart enough as is," Puttermesser said.

"Whyn't you let the kid answer for herself?"

Puttermesser took Cracow by the elbow and whispered, "They cut out her throat. Malignancy of the voicebox."

"Whew," Cracow said.

"Get going," Puttermesser ordered the golem, and led her to the ladies' room. "I told you not to come! I'm in enough hot water around here, I don't need you to make trouble."

The golem plucked a paper towel from the wall, fetched Puttermesser's ballpoint pen from the pocket of Puttermesser's cardigan (the golem was still wearing it), and wrote: "I will ameliorate your woe."

"I didn't say woe, I said hot water. *Trouble*. First kitsch, now rococo. Observe reality, can't you? Look, you're going to sit in front of that typewriter and that's it. If you can type half as well as you cook, fine. I don't care *what* you type. Stay out of my way. Write letters, it doesn't matter, but stay out of my way."

The golem wrote, "I hear and obey."

All day the golem, a model of diligence, sat at the typewriter and typed. Puttermesser, passing en route from one fruitless meeting to another, saw the sheets accumulating on the floor. Was Xanthippe writing a novel? a memoir? To whom, after all, did she owe a letter? The golem looked abstracted, rapt. Puttermesser was hoping to patch together, bit by bit, her bad fortune. The gossips ran from cubicle to cubicle, collecting the news: Turtelman's niece, an actress—she had most recently played a medieval leper, with a little bell, in a television costume drama—was engaged to the Mayor's cousin. Marmel's aunt had once stayed in the same hotel in Florida with Mrs. Minnie Mavett, the Mayor's elderly widowed adoptive mother. (The Mayor had been an adopted child, and campaigned with his wife and four natural children as a "lucky orphan.") Marmel and Turtelman were said to have married twin sisters; surely this was a symbolic way of marrying each other? Or else Marmel was married to a Boston blueblood, Turtelman to a climber from Great Neck. On the other hand, only Marmel was married; Turtelman was an austere bachelor. One of the secretaries in the Administrative Assistant's office had observed that Marmel, Turtelman, and the Mayor all wore identical rings; she denied they were school rings. Turtelman's "restructuring," moreover, had begun (according to Polly in Personnel) to assume telltale forms. He was becoming bolder and bolder. He was like some crazed plantation owner at harvest time, who, instead of cutting down the standing grain, cuts down the conscientious reapers. Or he was like a raving chessmaster who throws all the winning pieces in the fire. Or he was like a general who leads a massacre against his own best troops. All these images failed. Turtelman was destroying the Department of Receipts and Disbursements. What he looked for was not performance but loyalty. He was a mayoral appointee of rapacious nature conniving at the usual outrages of patronage; he was doing the Mayor's will. He did not love the democratic polity as much as he feared the Mayor. Ah, Walt Whitman was not in his kidneys. Plunder was.

Cracow, meanwhile, reported that several times Adam Marmel had telephoned for Puttermesser. It was urgent. "That new girl's no good, Ruth. I'm all in favor of hiring the handicapped, but when it comes to answering the telephone what's definitely needed is a larynx. I had to pick up every damn time. You think Marmel wants to put you back up there in the stratosphere?"

Puttermesser said nothing. Cracow thought women ought to keep their place; he took open satisfaction in Puttermesser's flight downward. He nagged her to tell him what Turtelman's special project was. "You'd rather do special projects for the higher-ups than date a nice guy like me," he complained. "At least let's have lunch." But Puttermesser sent the golem out to a delicatessen for sandwiches; it was a kosher delicatessen—Puttermesser thought the golem would care about a thing like that. By the middle of the afternoon the golem's typed sheets were a tall stack.

At a quarter to five Turtelman's bony acolyte came puffing in. "Mr. Turtelman lent me to Mr. Marmel just to give you this. I hope you appreciate I'm not normally anyone's delivery boy. You're never at your desk. You can't be reached by phone. You're not important enough to be incommunicado, believe me. Mr. Marmel wants you to prepare a portfolio for him on these topics toot sweet."

Marmel's memo:

Dear Ms. Puttermesser:

Please be good enough to supply me with the following at your earliest convenience. A list of the City's bank depositories. Average balance in each account for the last three years. List of contact people at banks—names, titles, telephone numbers. List of contacts for Department of Receipts and Disbursements (referred to below as "we," "our," and "us") in Office of Mayor, Department of Budget, relevant City Council committees, Office of Comptroller. Copies of all evaluation reports published during past year. Current organization chart showing incumbent, title, and salary for each of our Office Heads. Why do we not have any window poles? Where have all the window poles gone? How to get toilet paper and soap regularly replaced in executive washroom? What kind of Management Information System files do we have on the assessed value of City real estate? How effective was our last Investors' Tour? Old notes disclose visit to sewage disposal plant, helicopter ride, fireboat demonstration, lunch and fashion show for the ladies— how to win goodwill this year from these heavy pockets? What hot litigation should I know about in re our Quasi-Judicial Division?

It was the old story: the floundering new official perplexed and beleaguered. Puttermesser felt a touch of malicious pleasure in Marmel's memo; she had known it would come to this—Turtelman, having thrown her out, now discovered he could not clear a space for himself without the stirring of Puttermesser's little finger. Marmel, spurred by Turtelman (too high-and-mighty to ask on his own), had set out to pick Puttermesser's brain. He was appealing to Puttermesser to diaper him. Each item in Marmel's memo would take hours and hours to answer! Except for the window poles. Puttermesser could explain about the window poles in half a second.

"Stand by," she said to the bony acolyte. And to Xanthippe: "Take a letter!"

Mr. Adam Marmel
First Bursary Officer
Bureau of Summary Sessions
Department of Receipts and Disbursements
Municipal Building

Dear Mr. Marmel:

Window poles are swiped by the hottest and sweatiest secretaries. The ones located directly above the furnace room, for instance. Though lately the ones who jog at lunchtime are just as likely to pinch poles. When they get them they hide them. Check out the second-floor ladies' room.

The fresh air of candor is always needed whenever the oxygen of honest admission has been withdrawn. Precisely WHY ["Make that all capitals," Puttermesser said, dictating] have I been relieved of my position? Precisely WHY have you stepped into my job? Let us have some fresh air!

Yours sincerely,
R. Puttermesser, Esq.

The bony acolyte snatched the sheet directly from the golem's typewriter. "There's a lot more he wants answers to. You've left out practically everything."

"Window poles are everything," Puttermesser said. "The fresh air of candor is all." She observed—it was a small shock —that the golem's style had infected her.

The bony acolyte warned, "Fresh is right. You better answer the rest of what he wants answered."

"Go home," Puttermesser told the golem. "Home!"

During dinner in the little kitchen Puttermesser was nearly as silent as the golem. Injustice rankled. She paid no attention to the golem's scribblings. The nerve! The nerve! To throw her out and then come and pick her brain! "No more Swedish soufflé," she growled. "Cook something else for a change. And I'm getting tired of seeing you in my old sweater. I'll give you money, tomorrow go buy yourself some decent clothes."

"Tomorrow," the golem wrote, "I will again serve you at your place of employment."

But in the morning Puttermesser was lackadaisical; ambition had trickled away. What, after so much indignity, was there to be ambitious *for?* For the first time in a decade she came to the office late. "What's the special project, Ruth?" Cracow wanted to know right away. "The kid was burning up the typewriter yesterday. What is she anyhow, an illegal alien? She don't look like your ordinary person. Yemenite Israeli type? What is this, already she don't show up, it's only the second day on the job? The phone calls you missed! Memos piled up! That gal from Personnel back and forth two, three times! They're after you today, Ruth! The higher-ups! What's the special project, hah? And the kid leaves you high and dry!"

"She'll turn up." Puttermesser had given the golem a hundred and twenty dollars and sent her to Alexander's. "No taxis or else," Puttermesser said; but she knew the golem would head downtown to Delancey Street. The thronged Caribbean faces and tongues of the Lower East Side drew her; Xanthippe, a kind of foreigner herself, as even Cracow could see, was attracted to immigrant populations. Their tastes and adorations were hers. She returned with red and purple blouses, narrow skirts and flared pants of parrot-green and cantaloupe-orange, multicolored high-heeled plastic shoes, a sunflower-yellow plastic shoulder bag with six double sets of zippers, a pocket mirror, and a transparent plastic comb in its own peach tattersall plastic case.

"Hispanic absolutely," Cracow confirmed—Cracow the bigot—watching Xanthippe lay open boxes and bags.

But Puttermesser was occupied with a trio of memos. They appeared to originate with Marmel but were expressed through Polly, the Atropos of Personnel, she who had put aside her shears for the flurry of a thousand Forms, she who brooded like Shiva the Destroyer on a world of the lopped.

Memo One:

You are reported as having refused to respond to requests for information relating to Bureau business. You now are subject to conduct inquiry. Please obtain and fill out Form 10V, Q17, with particular reference to Paragraph L, and leave it *immediately* with Polly in Personnel.

Memo Two:

In consideration of your seniority, Commissioner Alvin Turtelman, having relieved you of Level Eleven status in the Bureau of Summary Sessions, Department of Receipts and Disbursements, due to insufficient control of bursary materials, weak administrative supervision as well as output insufficiency, has retained you at Level Four. However, your work shows continued decline. Lateness reported as of A.M. today. Fill out Below-Level-Eight Lateness Form 14TG. (Submit Form to Polly in Personnel.)

Memo Three:

As a result of a determination taken by Commissioner Alvin Turtelman in conjunction and in consultation with First Bursary Officer Adam Marmel, your Level Four appointment in the Department of Receipts and Disbursements is herewith terminated. Please submit Below-Level-Six Severance Form A97, Section 6, with particular reference to Paragraph 14b, to Polly in Personnel.

Severed! Sacked! Dismissed! Let go! Fired! And all in the space of three hours! "Output insufficiency," a lie! "Decline," a fiction! "Conduct inquiry"—like some insignificant clerk or window-pole thief! Late once in ten years and Cracow, litigious would-be lover, snitches to Polly, the Atropos, the Shiva, of Personnel! Who else but Cracow? Lies. Fabrications. Accusations. Marmel the hollow accuser. Absence of due process!

The Honorable Malachy Mavett
Mayor, City of New York
City Hall

Dear Mayor Mavett:
    Where is your pride, to appoint such men? Men who accuse without foundation? An accuser who seizes the job of the accused? Suspect! Turtelman wanted me out in order to get Marmel in! I stand for Intellect and Knowledge, they stand for Politics and Loyal Cunning. Hart Crane, poet of New York, his harp the Brooklyn Bridge, does that harp mean nothing to you? Is Walt

Whitman dead in your kidneys? Walt Whitman who cried out "numberless crowded streets, high growths of iron, slender, strong, light, splendidly uprising toward clear skies," who embraced "a million people—manners free and superb—open voices—hospitality . . . " Oh, Mayor Mavett, it is Injustice you embrace! You have given power to men for whom Walt Whitman is dead in their kidneys! This city of masts and spires opens its breast for Walt Whitman, and you feed it with a Turtelman and a Marmel! Ruth Puttermesser is despised, demoted, thrown away at last! Destroyed. Without work. Doer of nought, maker of nothing.

This letter remained locked inside Puttermesser's head. Cracow was trying hard not to look her way. He had already read Marmel's memos manifested through Polly the Destroyer; he had surely read them. He stood behind the golem's chair, attentive to her fingers galloping over the typewriter keys—including the newly lengthened one; how glad Puttermesser was that she had fixed it! "Hey Ruth, take a gander at this stuff. What's this kid *doing?* That's some so-called special project for Turtelman."

"The special project for Turtelman," Puttermesser said coldly, "is my vanquishment. My vanishing. My send-off and diminishment. So long, Leon. May you win your case against the mediocre universality of the human imagination."

"You been canned?"

"You know that."

"Well, when Polly walks in you figure what's up. You figure who's out."

"Beware of *Schadenfreude*, Leon. You could be next."

"Not me. I don't look for trouble. You look for trouble. I knew right away this whole setup with the kid was phony. She's typing up a craziness—whatever it is, Bureau business it isn't. You let in the crazies, you get what you expect."

At that moment—as Cracow's moist smile with its brown teeth turned and turned inside Cracow's dark mouth—a clarification came upon Puttermesser: no: a clarity. She was shut of a mystery. She understood; she saw.

"Home!" Puttermesser ordered the golem. Xanthippe gathered up her clothes and shoved the typewritten sheets into one of the blouse bags.

V. WHY THE GOLEM WAS CREATED; PUTTERMESSER'S PURPOSE

That night the golem cooked spaghetti. She worked barefoot. The fragrance of hot buttered tomato sauce and peppers rushed over a mound of shining porcelain strands. "What are you doing?" Puttermesser demanded; she saw the golem heaping up a second great batch. "Why are you so hungry?"

The golem looked a little larger today than she had yesterday.

Then Puttermesser remembered that it was in the nature of a golem to grow and grow. The golem's appetite was nevertheless worrisome—how long would it take for Xanthippe to grow out of over one hundred dollars' worth of clothes? Could only a Rothschild afford a golem? And what would the rate of growth be? Would the golem eventually have to be kept outdoors, so as not to crash through the ceiling? Was the golem of Prague finally reversed into lifelessness on account of its excessive size, or because the civic reforms it was created for had been accomplished?

Ah, how this idea glowed for Puttermesser! The civic reforms of Prague—the broad crannied city of Prague, Prague distinguished by numberless crowded streets, high growths of iron, masts and spires! The clock-tower of the Jewish Community House, the lofty peaked and chimneyed roof of the

Altneuschul! Not to mention Kafka's Castle. All that mani-
fold urban shimmer choked off by evil, corruption, the blood
libel, the strong dampened hearts of wicked politicos. The
Great Rabbi Judah Loew had undertaken to create his golem
in an unenlightened year, the dream of America just unfolding, far away, in all its spacious ardor; but already the seed of
New York was preparing in Europe's earth: inspiration of
city-joy, love for the comely, the cleanly, the free and the
new, mobs transmuted into troops of the blessed, citizens
bursting into angelness, sidewalks of alabaster, buses filled
with thrones. Old delicate Prague, swept and swept of sin,
giving birth to the purified daylight, the lucent genius, of New
York!

By now Puttermesser knew what she knew.

"Bring me my books," she ordered the golem. And read:

A vision of Paradise must accompany the signs. The
sacred formulae are insufficient without the trance of
ecstasy in which are seen the brilliance of cities and their
salvation through exile of heartlessness, disorder, and the
desolation of sadness.

A city washed pure. New York, city (perhaps) of seraphim.
Wings had passed over her eyes. Her arms around Rappoport's heavy *Times*, Puttermesser held to her breast heartlessness, disorder, the desolation of sadness, ten thousand knives,
hatred painted in the subways, explosions of handguns, bombs
in the cathedrals of transportation and industry, Pennsylvania
Station, Grand Central, Rockefeller Center, terror in the
broadcasting booths with their bustling equipment and seductive provincial voices, all the metropolitan airports assaulted,
the decline of the Civil Service, maggots in high management.
Rappoport's *Times*, repository of a dread freight! All the

same, carrying Rappoport's *Times* back to bed, Puttermesser had seen Paradise.

New York washed, reformed, restored.

"Xanthippe!"

The golem, who had been scrubbing spaghetti sauce off the dishes in a little cascade of water-thunder under the kitchen faucet, wiped her hands on her new orange blouse, snatched up ballpoint pen and notepad, and ran to Puttermesser.

Puttermesser asked, "When you woke into life what did you feel?"

"I felt like an embryo," the golem wrote.

"What did you know?"

"I knew why I was created," the golem wrote.

"Why were you created?"

"So that my mother should become what she was intended to become," the golem wrote.

"Bring me that stack of stuff you were fooling around with in the office," Puttermesser ordered, but the golem had already scampered off to the bedroom closet to rummage among her boxes and bags of new clothes.

So Puttermesser set aside her books about the history and nature of the genus golem and settled down to contemplate all the pages the golem had typed for two days in Puttermesser's sorrowful cubicle, shared with Cracow—the cubicle of her demotion, denigration, disgrace—in the Taxation Section of the Bureau of Summary Sessions of the Department of Receipts and Disbursements of the City of New York.

What the golem had composed was a *PLAN*. Puttermesser recognized everything in it. It was as if she had encountered this *PLAN* before—its very language. It was as if, in the instant it had occurred to her to make the golem, she had read the *PLAN* in some old scroll. Ah, here was a stale and restless truth: that she did not recollect the actual fabrication of the golem, that she had helplessly, without volition, come upon

Xanthippe in her bed as if the golem were some transient mirage, an aggressive imagining, or else a mere forward apparition—this had, with a wearisome persistence, been teasing at the edge of Puttermesser's medulla oblongata all along, ever since the first mulling of it on her desolate walk to the Y. It was like a pitcher that will neither fill nor pour out. But it was now as plain as solid earth itself that the golem was no apparition. Apparitions do not, in hideous public jargon, type up exhaustive practical documents concerning civic reform! Puttermesser knew what she knew—it unraveled before her in the distance, the *PLAN*, approaching, approaching, until it crowded her forebrain with its importuning force: how she had set Rappoport's *Times*, record of multiple chaos and urban misfortune, down on the floor beside the bed, where the *Theaetetus* already lay. How, with a speed born of fever and agitation, she had whirled from window sill to window sill, cracking open clay plant pots as though they were eggs, and scooping up the germinative yolks of spilling earth. How she had fetched it all up in her two palms and dumped it into the bathtub. How only a half-turn of the tap stirred earth to the consistency of mud—and how there then began the blissful shudder of Puttermesser's wild hands, the molding and the shaping, the caressing and the smoothing, the kneading and the fingering, the straightening and the rounding, but quickly, quickly, with detail itself (God is in the details) unachieved, blurred, completion deferred, the authentic pleasure of the precise final form of nostril and eyelid and especially mouth left for afterward. Into the hole of the unfinished face of clay Puttermesser pressed a tag of paper, torn from the blank upper margin of Rappoport's *Times*, on which she had written in her own spittle two oracular syllables. The syllables adhered and were as legible as if inscribed in light. Then Puttermesser raised up out of the tub the imponderous damp relentless clay of a young girl—a lifeless forked creature in the semblance of a girl—and smelled the smell of mud, and put her down in her own bed to dry. The small jar to that small weight loosened crumbs of earth wherever a limb was joined to the trunk, and where the neck was joined, and where the ears had their fragile connecting stems. The crumbs sprinkled down. They crept under Puttermesser's fingernails.

And all this Puttermesser performed (aha, now it beat in hindbrain and in forebrain, she saw it, she knew it again!) because of agitation and fever: because of the wilderness inside Rappoport's *Times*. Why should the despoiled misgoverned miscreant City not shine at dawn like washed stones? Tablets of civilization, engraved with ontological notations in an ancient tongue. Puttermesser craved. Her craving was to cleanse the wilderness; her craving was to excise every black instance of injustice; her craving was to erase outrage. In the middle of her craving—out of the blue—she formulated the PLAN.

She was thumbing it now, it was in her hands:

PLAN

FOR THE

RESUSCITATION,

REFORMATION,

REINVIGORATION

& REDEMPTION

OF THE

CITY OF NEW YORK

"Where did you get this?" Puttermesser demanded.

"I am your amanuensis," the golem wrote. "I express you. I copy and record you. Now it is time for you to accomplish your thought."

"Everyone has funny thoughts," Puttermesser croaked; an uneasiness heated her. She was afraid of the last page.

"No reality greater than thought," the golem wrote.

"Lay off the Middle Finnish. I want to hear the truth about all this. Where'd this stuff come from? You *couldn't* copy it, I never put any of it down."

The golem wrote: "Two urges seeded you. I am one, this is the other. A thought must claim an instrument. When you conceived your urge, simultaneously you conceived me."

"Not simultaneously," Puttermesser objected; perhaps the golem could not be trusted with chronology. She breathed outside history. Puttermesser re-imagined the electric moment exactly: the PLAN swimming like an inner cosmos into being, the mere solid golem an afterthought.

"No matter; I will serve your brain. I am your offspring, you are my mother. I am the execution of the grandeur of your principles. Grand design is my business. Leave visionary restoration to me." After which the golem put the ballpoint pen in her mouth and patiently sucked.

A fatigue seeped into Puttermesser; a tedium. It struck her that the golem was looking sly. She noticed that the seams along the armholes in the golem's orange blouse had begun to open. Growth. Enlargement. Swelling. Despite distraction Puttermesser read on. The PLAN, though it had originated in her own mind, nevertheless smacked of Marmel's lingo, Turtelman's patois. It appeared to derive, in truth, from the Formlanguage of Polly the Destroyer. A starkness penetrated Puttermesser; the dead words themselves depressed her. Her wrists shook. Was it not possible to dream a dream of City without falling into the mouth of the Destroyer? Behold the conservation of residential property through the exclusion of depreciating factors. Compute twelve hundred and fifty zoning codes. Note physical aspects. Social aspects. Retail and wholesale business. Manufacturing. Shipping. Single and multiple residences. Cultural institutions. Parks, public buildings, amusements, schools, universities, community objectives, rapidity and feasibility of transportation via streets and transit lines. Health, traffic, safety, public assembly conveniences. Sanitation. Prevention of slums. Transformation of slums. Eradication of poverty. Morality and obedience to law. Ordinances. Trust and pension funds. Treasury, public works, water. Public library. Police. Inspection. Councils and commissions. Welfare. Trustees. Revenue forecasting. Remote teleprocessing systems, computerized key-entry, restructuring of assessment districts, liens, senior-citizen rent-increase exemptions, delinquency centralization, corporate billings!

"My God," Puttermesser said.

"My mother has mastered and swallowed all of it," the golem wrote. "All of it is inside my mother's intelligence."

"I only meant—" Weak, Puttermesser wondered what it was she had meant. "Gardens and sunlight. Washed stones. Tablets. No; tables. Picnic tables."

Xanthippe stood nodding. The slyness powered her eyes. "My mother will become Mayor," she wrote.

The golem took the stack of typed sheets from Puttermesser's unquiet hands and held out the last page:

BY ORDER OF
RUTH PUTTERMESSER,
MAYOR
OF THE
CITY OF NEW YORK

"Drivel. Now you've gone too far. *I* never thought of that."

"Sleep on it," the golem wrote.

"That's *your* idea. You're the one who put that one in."

"Creator and created," the golem wrote, "merge," scribbling this with a shrug; the shrug made the ripped seams in her orange blouse open a little more.

The Honorable Malachy Mavett
Mayor
City Hall

Dear Mayor Mavett:
   It is not respectful of a citizen's conception of the
Mayor's office as "responsive" that you ignore my letter
about possible spoils and other abuses. Still less is it
respectful of me as a living human being and as a (former, now dismissed) Civil Servant. Shame! Shame!
                    Very sincerely yours,
              THE HONORABLE RUTH PUTTERMESSER

This letter too remained locked inside Puttermesser's head.
The signature was experimental—just to see what it looked
like.
   "No use, no use," the golem wrote on her notepad. "Mayor
Puttermesser, by contrast, will answer all letters."

VI. MAYOR PUTTERMESSER

And so Puttermesser becomes Mayor of New York. The
"and so" encloses much—but not so much as one might think.
It is only a way of hastening Puttermesser's blatant destiny, of
avoiding—never mind that God is in the details!—a more
furrowed account of how the golem, each day imperceptibly
enlarging, goes about gathering signatures for a citizens' petition. The golem is above all a realist; Puttermesser will run as
an independent. There is not the minutest hope that the
county leaders of either the Democratic or the Republican
party will designate, as preferred candidate for Mayor of the
City of New York, Ruth Puttermesser, Esq., a currently un-

employed attorney put out in the street, so to speak, by Commissioner Alvin Turtelman of the Department of Receipts and Disbursements, in conjunction and in consultation with First Bursary Officer Adam Marmel. The golem is Puttermesser's campaign manager. She has burst out of all her new clothes, and has finally taken to extra-large men's denim overalls bought in the Army-Navy store on the corner of Suffolk and Delancey. The golem's complexion has coarsened a little. It is somehow redder, and the freckles on her forehead, when gazed at by an immobile eye, appear to have the configuration of a handful of letters from a generally unrecognizable alphabet:

$$† \xi \ltimes$$

Puttermesser has not failed to take note of how these letters, *aleph, mem,* and *tav,* in their primal North Semitic form, read from right to left, have extruded themselves with greater and greater clarity just below the golem's hairline. Puttermesser attributes this to pressure of the skin as the golem gains in height and thickness. She orders the golem to cut bangs. Though she is periodically alarmed at what a large girl Xanthippe is growing into, otherwise Puttermesser is pleased by her creation. Xanthippe is cheerful and efficient, an industrious worker. She continues to be a zealous cook. She remains unsure about time (occasionally she forgets that Wednesday intrudes between Tuesday and Thursday, and she has not quite puzzled out the order of all the months, though she has it splendidly fixed that November will embrace what has now become the sun of Puttermesser's firmament—Election Day); she is sometimes cocky; often intrepid; now and then surly; mainly she smiles and smiles. She can charm a signature out of anyone. At her own suggestion she wears around her neck a card that reads DEAF-MUTE, and with this card dangling on her bosom, in overalls, she scrambles up and down tenement steps as far away as Bensonhurst and Canarsie, in and out of elevators of East Side and West Side apartment buildings. She churns through offices, high schools and universities (she has visited Fordham, L.I.U., Pace, N.Y.U., Baruch College, Columbia; she has solicited the teaching staffs of Dalton, Lincoln, Brearley, John Dewey, Julia Richman, Yeshiva of Flatbush, Fieldston, Ramaz, as well as Puttermesser's own alma mater, Hunter High), supermarkets, cut-rate drugstores, subway stations, the Port Authority bus terminal. Wherever there are signers to be found, the golem appears with her ballpoint pen.

The petition is completed. The golem has collected fourteen thousand five hundred and sixty-two more signatures than the law calls for.

All this must be recorded as lightly and swiftly as possible; a dry patch to be gotten through, perhaps via a doze or a skip. For Puttermesser herself it is much more wretched than a mere dry patch. She suffers. Her physiological responses are: a coldness in the temples, blurring of the eyes, increased periodontic difficulties. She is afflicted with frequent diarrhea. Her spine throbs. At night she weeps. But she keeps on. Xanthippe gives her no peace, urges her to rephrase her speeches with an ear for the lively, insists that she sport distinctive hats, glossy lipstick, even contact lenses (Puttermesser, edging into middle age, already owns reading glasses).

The golem names Puttermesser's party as follows: Independents for Socratic and Prophetic Idealism—ISPI for short. A graphic artist is hired to devise a poster. It shows an apple tree with a serpent in it. The S in ISPI is the serpent. Puttermesser has promised to transform the City of New York into Paradise. She has promised to cast out the serpent. On Election Day, Malachy ("Matt") Mavett, the incumbent, is routed. Of the three remaining candidates, two make poor showings. Puttermesser is triumphant.

Puttermesser is now the Mayor of the City of New York! Old ardors and itches wake in her. She recites to herself: Justice, justice shalt thou pursue. Malachy ("Matt") Mavett takes his wife and family to Florida, to be near Mrs. Minnie Mavett, his adoptive mother. He is no longer a lucky orphan. He gets a job as a racetrack official. It is a political job, but he is sad all the same. His wife bears his humiliation gracelessly. His children rapidly acquire accents that do not mark them as New Yorkers. Turtelman and Marmel vanish into rumor. They are said to be with the F.B.I. in Alaska, with the C.I.A. in Indonesia. They are said to have relocated at Albany. They are said to be minor factotums in the Federal Crop Insurance Corporation, with offices in Sourgrass, Iowa. They are said to have mediocre positions in the Internal Revenue Service, where they will not be entitled to Social Security. They are said to have botched a suicide pact. No one knows what has become of Turtelman and Marmel. But Puttermesser is relieved; she herself, by means of a memo from City Hall, has dismissed them. Turtelman and Marmel are sacked! Let go! Fired!

Malachy ("Matt") Mavett, following protocol, telephones to congratulate Puttermesser on her victory. But he confesses to bafflement. Where has Puttermesser come from? An ordinary drone from the Bureau of Summary Sessions of the Department of Receipts and Disbursements! How can she, "an unknown," he asks, "a political nonentity," have won the public over so handily? Puttermesser reminds him that some months ago she wrote him a letter asking for justice, condemning patronage and spoils. "You did not reply," she accuses him in a voice hoarse from speech-making. The ex-Mayor does not remember any letter.

Though Puttermesser is disconcerted by the move to Gracie Mansion (in her dreams her mother is once again rolling up winter rugs and putting down summer rugs in the wide sun-periled apartment on the Grand Concourse), the golem immediately chooses the most lavish bedroom in the Mayor's residence for herself. It contains an antique dresser with gryphon feet and a fourposter arched by a lofty tester curtained in white velvet. Old brass bowls glint on the dressertop. The golem fills one whole closet with fresh overalls. She wanders about studying the paintings and caressing the shining banister. She exhorts Puttermesser to rejoice that she no longer has her old suspicious landlord on East Seventy-first Street to worry about. Millions of citizens are her landlord now!

Puttermesser cannot pay attention to the golem's sprightliness. She is in a frenzy over the job of appointing commissioners and agency heads. She implores Xanthippe to keep away from City Hall—the campaign is over, she will only distract from business. The new Mayor intends to recruit noble psyches and visionary hearts. She is searching for the antithesis of Turtelman and Marmel. For instance: she yearns after Wallace Stevens—insurance executive of probity during office hours, enraptured poet at dusk. How she would like to put Walt Whitman himself in charge of the Bureau of Summary Sessions, and have Shelley take over Water Resource Development—Shelley whose principle it is that poets are the legislators of mankind! William Blake in the Fire Department. George Eliot doing Social Services. Emily Brontë over at Police, Jane Austen in Bridges and Tunnels, Virginia Woolf and Edgar Allan Poe sharing Health. Herman Melville overseeing the Office of Single Room Occupancy Housing. "*Integer vitae scelerisque purus*," the golem writes on her notepad, showing off. "That's the ticket," Puttermesser agrees, "but what am I supposed to do, chase around town like Diogenes with a lantern looking for an honest man?" Xanthippe writes philosophically, "The politics of Paradise is no longer politics." "The politics of Paradise is no longer Paradise," Puttermesser retorts; "don't annoy me anyhow, I have to get somebody fast for Receipts and Disbursements." "You could promote Cracow," the golem writes. "I already have. I moved him over to Bronx Landfill and Pest Control. That's two levels up. He's got a good idea for winter, actually— wants to convert that garbage mountain out near the bay to a ski jump. And he's stopped asking me out. Thank God he's scared of dating the Mayor." "If you would seek commis- sioners of integrity and rosy cleverness," the golem writes, "fashion more of my kind." Fleetingly, Puttermesser consid- ers this; she feels tempted. The highest echelons of City man- agement staffed by multiple members of the genus golem! Herself the creator, down to the last molecule of ear-wax, of every commissioner, deputy, bureau chief, executive director! Every mayoral assistant, subordinate, underling, a golem! She looks over at Xanthippe. Twice already Xanthippe has quar- reled with the Mansion's official cook. The cook has refused to follow the golem's recipes. "One is enough," Puttermesser says, and hurries down the subway and off to City Hall.

Despite its odious language reminiscent of Turtelman and Marmel, Puttermesser repeatedly consults the

PLAN

FOR THE
RESUSCITATION,
REFORMATION,
REINVIGORATION
& REDEMPTION
OF THE
CITY OF NEW YORK.

She blames Xanthippe for such a preposterous text: only two days spent in the Bureau of Summary Sessions, and the golem has been infected by periphrasis, pleonasm, and ambagious tautology. But behind all that there glimmers a loveliness. To Puttermesser's speeding eye, it is like the spotted sudden flank of a deer disturbing a wood. There *will* be resuscitation! There *will* be redemption!

And it begins. Mayor Puttermesser sends the golem out into the City. At first she tends to hang out among the open-air stalls of Delancey Street, but Puttermesser upbraids her for parochialism; she instructs the golem to take subways and buses—no taxis—out to all the neighborhoods in all the boroughs. It goes without saying that a robust reformist administration requires a spy. The golem returns with aching tales of what she has seen among the sordid and the hopeless; sometimes she even submits a recommendation on a page of her notepad. Puttermesser does not mind. Nothing the golem reports is new to Mayor Puttermesser. What is new is the discovery of the power of office. Wrongdoing and bitterness can be overturned: it is only a matter of using the power Puttermesser owns.

Crowds of self-seeking importuners float up the steps of City Hall; Mayor Puttermesser shoos them away. She admits visionary hearts only. She tacks signs up all around her desk: NO MORE SPOILS QUOTA. MERIT IS SWEETER THAN GOLD. WHAT YOU ARE, NOT WHOM YOU KNOW.

Lost wallets are daily being returned to their owners. Now it is really beginning—the money and credit cards are always intact. The golem ascends from the subway at Sixty-eighth and Lexington (this is the very corner where Puttermesser's alma mater, Hunter High, used to stand), looking slightly larger than the day before, but also irradiated. The subways have been struck by beauty. Lustrous tunnels unfold, mile after mile. Gangs of youths have invaded the subway yards at night and have washed the cars clean. The wheels and windows have been scrubbed by combinations of chemicals; the long seats have been fitted with velour cushions of tan and blue. Each car shines like a bullet. The tiles that line the stations are lakes of white; the passengers can cherish their own reflections in the walls. Every Thursday afternoon the youths who used to terrorize the subways put on fresh shirts and walk out into Central Park, reconnoitering after a green space; then, they dance. They have formed themselves into dancing clubs, and crown one another's heads with clover pulled up from the sweet ground. Foliage is browning, Thursday afternoons grow cold and dusky. But the youths who used to terrorize the subways are whirling in rings over darkening lawns.

The streets are altered into garden rows: along the curbs, between sidewalk and road, privet hedges shake their little leaves. The open sanitation carts are bright, like a string of scarlet chariots. They are drawn by silent horses who sniff among the new hedges. Flutes and clarinets announce the coming of the cart procession every day at noon, and children scramble to pick up every nub of cigarette or scrap of peel or paper wrapper, pressing with fistfuls toward the singing flutes and gravely marching horses, whose pairs of high nostrils flare outward like trumpets.

The great cargo trucks still spill into the intersections, carrying bolts of cloth, oranges, fowl, refrigerators, lamps, pianos, cards of buttons, lettuces, boxes of cereal, word processors, baby carriages, pillowcases with peacocks imprinted on them; some deliver uptown, others downtown; they pant and rumble freely, unimpeded; buses and taxis overtake them effortlessly. Except for fire engines and ambulances, there are no other motored vehicles. Little girls dare, between buses, to jump rope in the middle of the street. Some roads, though, have been lushly planted, so that lovers seek them out to hide in one another's breast. The tall grasses and young maples of the planted roads are haunted by pretzel sellers, hot-chestnut peddlers, hawkers of books in wheelbarrows. The children are often indoors after school, carpentering bookshelves. The libraries are lit all night, and the schools are thronged in the evenings by administrative assistants from the great companies, learning Spanish, Portuguese, Russian, Hebrew, Korean, and Japanese. There are many gardeners now, and a hundred urban gardening academies. There is unemployment among correction officers; numbers of them take gardening jobs. No one bothers to drag the steel shutters down over storefronts after closing. The Civil Service hums. Intellect and courtliness are in the ascendancy. Mayor Puttermesser has staffed the Department of Receipts and Disbursements with intelligent lawyers, both women and men, who honor due process. Turtelman and Marmel are replaced by visionary hearts. Never again will an accuser take the job of the accused, as Marmel did with Puttermesser! There is no more rapaciousness in the Bureau of Summary Sessions.

A little-known poet who specializes in terza rima is put in charge of Potter's Field. For each sad burial there, she composes a laudatory ode; even the obscure dead are not expendable or forlorn. The parks, their arbors and fields, are speckled with wide-mouthed terra-cotta urns; no one injures them. Far away in the Bronx, the grape-wreathed heads of wine gods are restored to the white stelae of the Soldiers' Monument, and the bronze angel on top of the Monument's great stone needle glistens. Nothing is broken, nothing is despoiled. No harm comes to anything or anyone. The burnt-out ruins of Brownsville and the South Bronx burst forth with spinneys of pines and thorny locusts. In their high secret pride, the slums undo themselves: stoops sparkle, new factories and stores buzz, children gaze down in gladness at shoes newly bought, still unscratched; the shoe stores give away balloons, and the balloons escape to the sky. Everywhere former louts and loiterers, muggers and thieves, addicts and cardsharps are doing the work of the world, absorbed, transformed. The biggest City agency is what used to be called Welfare; now it is the Department of Day Play, and delivers colored pencils and finger paints and tambourines to nurseries clamorous as bee-loud glades, where pianos shake the floors, and story-tellers dangle toddlers in suspense from morning to late afternoon, when their parents fetch them home to supper. Everyone is at work. Lovers apply to the City Clerk for marriage licenses. The Bureau of Venereal Disease Control has closed down. The ex-pimps are learning computer skills.

Xanthippe's heels have begun to hang over the foot of her fourposter bed in Gracie Mansion. The golem is worn out. She lumbers from one end of the City to the other every day, getting ideas. Mayor Puttermesser is not disappointed that the golem's ideas are mainly unexciting. The City is at peace. It is in the nature of tranquility—it is in the nature of Paradise—to be pacific; tame; halcyon. Oh, there is more to relate of how Mayor Puttermesser, inspired by the golem, has resuscitated, reformed, reinvigorated and redeemed the City of New York! But this too must be left to dozing and skipping. It is essential to record only two reflections that especially engage Mayor Puttermesser. The first is that she notices how the City, tranquil, turns toward the conventional and the orderly. It is as if tradition, continuity, propriety blossom of themselves: old courtesies, door-holding, hat-tipping, a thousand pleases and pardons and thank-yous. Something in the grain of Paradise is on the side of the expected. Sweet custom rules. The City in its redeemed state wishes to conserve itself. It is a rational daylight place; it has shut the portals of night.

Puttermesser's second reflection is about the golem. The coming of the golem animated the salvation of the City, yes—but who, Puttermesser sometimes wonders, is the true golem? Is it Xanthippe or is it Puttermesser? Puttermesser made Xanthippe; Xanthippe did not exist before Puttermesser made her: that is clear enough. But Xanthippe made Puttermesser Mayor, and Mayor Puttermesser too did not exist before. And that is just as clear. Puttermesser sees that she is the golem's golem.

In the newborn peaceable City, Xanthippe is restless. She is growing larger. Her growth is frightening. She can no longer fit into her overalls. She begins to sew together pairs of sheets for a toga.

VII. RAPPOPORT'S RETURN

On a late spring afternoon about halfway through her mayoral term, and immediately after a particularly depressing visit to the periodontist (she who had abolished crime in the subways was unable to stem gum disease in the hollow of her own jaw), Puttermesser came home to Gracie Mansion to find Rappoport waiting in her private sitting room.

"Hey, you've got some pretty tough security around here. I had a hell of a time getting let in," Rappoport complained.

"Last time I saw you," Puttermesser said, "you had no trouble letting yourself out."

"How about we just consider that water under the bridge, Ruth, what do you say?"

"You walked out on me. In the middle of the night."

"You were liking Socrates better than me," Rappoport said.

"Then why are you back?"

"My God, Ruth, look who you've become! I can't pass through New York without seeing the Mayor, can I? Ruth," he said, spreading his impressive nostrils, "I've thought about you a lot since the election. We read all about you up in Toronto."

"You and Mrs. Rappoport?"

"Oh come on, let's give it another try. Not that I don't understand you have to be like Caesar's wife. Above susp—"

"I have to be Caesar," Puttermesser broke in.

"Well, even Caesar gives things another try."

"You're no Cleopatra," Puttermesser said.

There was a distant howl; it was the cook. She was fighting with the golem again. In a moment Xanthippe stood in the doorway, huge and red, weeping.

"Leave that woman alone. She'll cook what she'll cook, you can't tell her anything different," Puttermesser scolded. "She runs a strictly kosher kitchen and that's enough. Go and wash your face."

"Plump," Rappoport said, staring after Xanthippe in her toga. "Right out of Caesar's Forum."

"A growing girl. She wears what she pleases."

"Who is she?"

"I adopted her."

"I like a big girl like that." Rappoport stood up. "The town looks terrific. I came to congratulate you, Ruth."

"Is that why you came?"

"It turns out. Only I figured if you could bring a whole city back to life—"

"There are some things, Morris, that even the Mayor can't revive."

Rappoport, his briefcase under his arm, wheeled and hesitated. "It didn't make it through the move? My avocado tree that I grew from a pit in Toronto? It was doing fine in your old apartment."

"I don't have it any more."

"Aha, you wanted to dispose of me lock, stock, and barrel. You got rid of every symptom and sign. The least bit of green leaf—"

"All my plants are gone."

"No kidding. What happened?"

"I took their earth and made a golem."

Rappoport, flaunting his perfect teeth under his mustache, laughed out loud. In the middle of his laughter his head suddenly fell into the kind of leaning charm Puttermesser recalled from long ago, when they had first become lovers; it almost made her relent.

"Goodbye, Ruth. I really do congratulate you on civic improvement." Rappoport held out his hand. "It's one terrific town, I mean it. Utopia. Garden of Eden. In Toronto they run articles on you every day."

"You can stay for dinner if you like," Puttermesser offered. "Though I've got a meeting right after—municipal bonds. Myself, it's eat and get on down to City Hall."

Someone had seized Rappoport's outstretched hand and was shaking it; it was not Puttermesser. Xanthippe, practiced politician, her wide cheeks refreshed and soap-fragrant, had sped forward out of nowhere. Rappoport looked stunned; he looked interested. He slipped his fingers out of the golem's grasp and moved them upward against her chest, to catch hold of the card that twirled there: DEAF-MUTE.

"That's awfully generous of you, Ruth, adopting someone like that. You're a wonderful person. We really ought to get together again. I *will* stay for a bite, if you don't mind."

The golem did not bring her ballpoint to the table. She dealt with her soup spoon as if it were her enemy, the cook. Disgruntled, she heaped a fourth helping of mashed potatoes onto her plate. But her eye was on Rappoport, and her mouth was round with responsiveness: was it his teeth? was it his reddish mustache, turning gray? was it his wide welcoming nostrils? was it his briefcase bulging with worldly troubles?

Rappoport was talkative. His posture was straight-backed and heroic: he told of his last clandestine trip to Moscow, and of the turmoil of the oppressed.

When Puttermesser returned at midnight from the meeting on municipal bonds, the golem was asleep in her fourposter bed, her heels thrust outward in their pink socks over the footboard, and Rappoport was snoring beside her.

Eros had entered Gracie Mansion.

VIII. XANTHIPPE LOVESICK

Consider now Puttermesser's situation. What happens to an intensely private mind when great celebrity unexpectedly invades it? Absorbed in the golem's *PLAN* and its consequences—consequences beyond the marveling at, so gradual, plausible, concrete, and sensible are they, grounded in a policy of civic sympathy and urban reasonableness—Puttermesser does not readily understand that she induces curiosity and applause. She has, in fact, no expectations; only desires as strong and as strange as powers. Her desires are pristine, therefore acute; clarity is immanent. Before this inward illumination of her desires (rather, of the *PLAN*'s desires), everything else—the clash of interests that parties, races, classes, are said to give rise to—falls away into purposelessness. Another way of explaining all this is to say that Mayor Puttermesser finds virtue to be intelligible. Still another way of explaining is to say that every morning she profoundly rejoices. There is fruitfulness everywhere. Into the chaos of the void (defeat, deception, demoralization, loss) she has cast a divinely clarifying light. Out of a dunghill she has charmed a verdant citadel. The applause that reaches her is like a seasound at the farthest edge of her brain; she both hears it and does not hear it. Her angelic fame—the fame of a purifying angel—is virtue's second face. Fame makes Puttermesser happy, and at the same time it brings a forceful sense of the penultimate, the tentative, the imperiled.

It is as if she is waiting for something else: for some conclusion, or resolution, or unfolding.

The golem is lovesick. She refuses to leave the Mansion. No more for her the daily voyage into the broad green City as

the Mayor's ambassador and spy. She removes the DEAF-MUTE
card and substitutes another: CONTEMPLATIVE. Puttermesser
does not smile at this: she is not sure whether it is meant to be
a joke. There is too much gloom. There are hints of conspiracy. Anyhow the golem soon takes off the new sign. In the
intervals between Rappoport's appearances Xanthippe lan-
guishes. Rappoport comes often—sometimes as often as three
or four times a week. Xanthippe, moping, thumps out to greet
him, trailing a loose white tail of her toga; she escorts him
straight into her bedroom. She turns on the record player that
Rappoport has brought her as a birthday gift. She is two years
old and insatiable. God knows what age she tells her lover.

Rappoport steals out of the golem's bedroom with the daz-
zled inward gaze of a space traveler.

The Mayor upbraids Xanthippe: "It's enough. I don't want
to see him around here. Get rid of him."

Xanthippe writes: "Jealousy!"

"I'm tired of hearing complaints from the cook. This is
Gracie Mansion, it's not another kind of house."

"Jealousy! He used to be yours."

"You're stirring up a scandal."

"He brings me presents."

"If you keep this up, you'll spoil everything."

"My mother has purified the City."

"Then don't foul it."

"I am in contemplation of my future."

"Start contemplating the present! Look out the window!
Fruitfulness! Civic peace! You saw it happening. You caused
it."

"I can tear it all down."

"You were made to serve and you know it."

"I want a life of my own. My blood is hot."

The Mansion thickens with erotic airs. Heavy perfumes
float. Has Rappoport journeyed to mysterious islands to offer

the golem these lethargic scents, these attars of weighty drooping petals? The golem has discarded her sewn-together sheets
and looms with gemlike eyes in darkling passageways,
wrapped in silks, vast saris that skim the carpets as she goes;
each leg is a pillar wound in a bolt of woven flowers.

The summer deepens. A dry dust settles on the leaves in the
Bronx Botanical Gardens, and far away the painted carousels
of Brooklyn cry their jollities.

The Mayor: "I notice Rappoport hasn't been around
lately."

Xanthippe writes: "He left."

"Where?"

"He clouded over his destination. Vienna. Rome. Jerusalem. Winnipeg. What do I care? A man of low position.
Factotum of refugee philanthropy, twelve bosses over him."

"What happened?"

"I wore him out."

"I need you right away," Puttermesser urges. "We're putting in new tiles on the subway line out toward Jamaica
Avenue. With two-color portraits baked right into the glaze—
Thoreau, Harriet Beecher Stowe, Emerson so far. You can
decide who else."

"No."

"You haven't been anywhere in months."

"My mother speaks the truth. I thirst for the higher world.
Office and rank. Illustrious men."

Puttermesser is blighted with melancholy. She fears. She
foresees. In spite of fruitfulness and civic peace (rather, on
their account), it is beginning to be revealed to her what her
proper mayoral duty directs.

She does nothing.

In pity, she waits. Sometimes she forgets. How long did the
Great Rabbi Judah Loew of Prague wait, how often did he
forget? There are so many distinguished visitors. The Em-

peror of Japan takes the elevator to the top of the Empire State Building. Puttermesser gives an astronaut a medal on the steps of City Hall; he has looked into the bosom of Venus. The mayors of Dublin, San Juan, and Tel Aviv arrive. In the Blue Room, Puttermesser holds a news conference about interest rates. She explains into the television cameras that the City of New York, in its abundance, will extend interest-free loans to the Federal government in Washington.

Now and then Xanthippe disappears. She does not return to the Mansion at night. Frequently her fourposter stands empty.

Early one morning, the golem, her eyes too polished, her cheeks too red, her silk windings torn, the tiny letters on her forehead jutting like raw scars, thumps home.

"Four days gone without a word!" Puttermesser scolds.

Xanthippe writes impatiently: "Been down to Florida."

"Florida!"

"Been to visit ex-Mayor Malachy ('Matt') Mavett."

"What for?"

"Remember Marmel?"

"What's this about?"

"Been out West to visit him. Him and Turtelman."

"What *is* this?"

But Puttermesser knows.

There are curious absences, reports of exhaustion, unexplained hospitalizations. The new Commissioner of Receipts and Disbursements whispers to Puttermesser, in confidence, that he will divorce his wife. His eyeballs seem sunken, his lips drop back into a hollow face. He has lost weight overnight. He will not say what the trouble is. He resigns. The Executive Director of the Board of Education resigns. It is divulged that he suffers from catarrh and is too faint to stand. The Commissioner of the Department of Cultural Affairs has been struck stone-deaf by a horrible sound, a kind of exultant hiss; he will not say what it was. The City's managers and executives all appear to sicken together: commissioner after commissioner, department after department. Puttermesser's finest appointments—felled; depleted. There is news of an abortion in Queens. A pimp sets himself up in business on Times Square again, in spite of the cherry trees the Department of Sanitation has planted there; the Commissioner of Sanitation himself stalks under the hanging cherries, distracted, with a twisted spine and the start of a hunch. Two or three of the proud young men of the dancing clubs defect and return to mugging in the subways. The City's peace is unraveling. The commissioners blow their noses into bloody tissues, drive their little fingers into their ears, develop odd stammers, instigate backbiting among underlings.

The golem thirsts.

"Stay home," the Mayor pleads. "Stay out of the City."

The golem will no longer obey. She cannot be contained. "My blood is hot," Xanthippe writes; she writes for the last time. She tosses her ballpoint pen into the East River, back behind the Mansion.

IX. THE GOLEM DESTROYS HER MAKER

Mayor Puttermesser's reputation is ebbing. The cost of municipal borrowing ascends. A jungle of graffiti springs up on the white flanks of marble sculptures inside museums; Attic urns are smashed. Barbarians cruise the streets. O New York! O lost New York!

Deputy commissioners and their secretaries blanch at the sound of a heavy footstep. Morning and afternoon the golem lumbers from office to office, searching for high-level managers. In her ragged sari brilliant with woven flowers, her great head garlanded, drenched in a density of musky oils, Xanthippe ravishes prestigious trustees, committee chairmen, council members, borough presidents, the Second Deputy Comptroller's three assistants, the Director of the Transit Authority, the Coordinator of Criminal Justice, the Chief of the Office of Computer Plans and Controls, the Head of Intergovernmental Relations, the Chancellor of the City University, the Rector of the Art Commission, even the President of the Stock Exchange! The City is diseased with the golem's urge. The City sweats and coughs in her terrifying embrace. The City is in the pincer of the golem's love, because Xanthippe thirsts, she thirsts, she ravishes and ravages, she ambushes management level after management level. There is no Supervising Accountant or Secretary to the Minority Leader who can escape her electric gaze.

Sex! Sex! The golem wants sex! Men in high politics! Lofty officials! Elevated bureaucrats!

Mayor Puttermesser is finished. She can never be re-elected. She is a disgrace; her Administration is wrecked. Distrust. Desolation. It is all over for Mayor Puttermesser and the life of high politics. The prisons are open again. The press howls. Mayor Puttermesser is crushed. The golem has destroyed her utterly.

X. THE GOLEM SNARED

Puttermesser blamed herself. She had not forestalled this devastation. She had not prepared for it; she had not acted. She had seen what had to be done, and put it off and put it off. Dilatory. She could not say to herself that she was ignorant; hadn't she read in her books, a thousand times, that a golem will at length undo its creator? The turning against the creator is an "attribute" of a golem, comparable to its speechlessness, its incapacity for procreation, its soullessness. A golem has no soul, therefore cannot die—rather, it is returned to the elements of its making.

Xanthippe without a soul! Tears came to Puttermesser, her heart in secret shook. She was ready to disbelieve. A golem cannot procreate? Ah, but its blood is as hot as human blood. Hotter! A golem lusts tremendously, as if it would wrest the flame of further being from its own being. A golem, an earthen thing of packed mud, having laid hold of life against all logic and natural expectation, yearns hugely after the generative, the fructuous. Earth is the germ of all fertility: how then would a golem not dream itself a double? It is like a panting furnace that cries out for more and more fuel, that spews its own firebrands to ignite a successor-fire. A golem cannot procreate! But it has the will to; the despairing will; the violent will. Offspring! Progeny! The rampaging energies of Xanthippe's eruptions, the furious bolts and convulsions of her visitations—Xanthippe, like Puttermesser herself, longs for daughters! Daughters that can never be!

Shall the one be condemned by the other, who is no different?

Yet Puttermesser weeps. The golem is running over the City. She never comes home at all now. A ferry on its way from the Battery to Staten Island is terrorized; some large creature, bat or succubus, assaults the captain and causes him to succumb. Is it Xanthippe? Stories about "a madwoman on the loose, venomous against authority" ("unverifiable," writes the City Hall Bureau of the *Times*) wash daily over Mayor Puttermesser's desk. The secret chamber where sleeps the President of the Chase Manhattan Bank has had its windows brutally smashed; a bit of flowered silk clings to the jagged glass.

Xanthippe! Xanthippe! Puttermesser calls in her heart.

Every night pickets parade in front of Gracie Mansion, with torches and placards:

MAYOR PUTTERMESSER WHAT HAS HAPPENED TO THE SUBWAYS?

HIGH HOPES THE HIGH ROAD TO HELL.

SHE WHO SPARKED SNUFFED.

PUTTERMESSER'S BITTER MESSES.

RUTHIE WITH SUCH A DOWN WE NEEDED YOUR UP?

FROM SMASH HIT TO SMASH.

KAPUT-TERMESSER!

Every day there are speakers on the steps of City Hall, haranguing; when the police chase them, they vanish for ten minutes and reappear. Mobs bubble, hobble, guffaw.

Puttermesser composes a letter to ex-Mayor Malachy ("Matt") Mavett:

> Gracie Mansion
> City of New York

Dear Matt [she permits herself this liberty]:

My campaign manager's recent Florida visit may have caused you some distress. I did not authorize it. Your defeat via the ballot box, which eliminated the wrong-doers Turtelman and Marmel from City officialdom, was satisfaction enough. Please excuse any personal indignities my campaign manager (who is now on my personal staff) may have inflicted. She expresses her nature but cannot assume responsibility for it.

Dilatory! Procrastinator! Imaginary letters! Puttermesser's tears go on falling.

Gracie Mansion
City of New York

Dear Morris:
   Please come.
          In friendship
          Ruth

She hands this to one of the window-pole thieves to mail. In a few days it brings Rappoport, out of breath, his once-pouting briefcase hollow, caved in; Rappoport himself is hollow, his stout throat caved in, as if he had ejected his Adam's apple. His nose and chin, and the furless place between his eyebrows, have a papery cast. His beautiful teeth are nicked. His mustache looks squirrelly, gray.

"Xanthippe's left home," Puttermesser announces.

"You're the Mayor. Call the Missing Persons Bureau."

"Morris. Please."

"What do you want?"

"Bring her back."

"Me?"

"You can do it."

"How?"

"Move in."

"What? Here? In Gracie Mansion?"

"In Xanthippe's bed. Morris. Please. She likes you. You're the one who started her off."

"She got too big for her britches. In more than a manner of speaking, if you don't mind my saying so. What d'you mean, started her off?"

"You excited her."

"That's not my fault."

"You created desire. Morris, bring her back. You can do it."

"What for? I've had enough. No more. Drained. Drained, believe me, Ruth."

"Lie in her bed. Just once."

"What's in it for me? I didn't come back to this rotten town for the sake of a night's sleep in Gracie Mansion. The novelty's worn off. The bloom is no longer on the rose, you follow? Besides, you've gone downhill, Ruth, did you see those pickets out there?" He shows her his sleeve—two buttons ripped off. "They treated me like a scab, walking in here—"

"Just lie down in her bed, Morris. That's all I'm asking."

"No."

"I'll make it worth your while."

"What're you getting at? You're getting at something."

"You're a fund-raiser by profession," Puttermesser says meditatively; a strangeness rises in her. A noxious taste.

"Something like that. There's a lot of different things I do."

"That's right. Plenty of experience. You're qualified for all sorts of fine spots."

"I'm qualified for what?"

"The truth is," Puttermesser says slowly, "I'm in possession of a heap of resignations. Several of my commissioners," Puttermesser says slowly, "have fallen ill."

"I hear there's typhoid in some of those buildings along Bruckner Boulevard. What've you got, an epidemic? I heard cholera in Forest Hills."

"Rumors," Puttermesser spits out. "People love to badmouth. That's what makes the City go down. The banks are leaving, nobody worries about *that*. I'm talking resignations. *Openings*, Morris. You can take your pick, in fact. How about the Department of Investigation? Run the Inspectors General. Or I can appoint you judge. How about Judge of the Criminal Court? Good spot, good pay. Prestige, God knows. Look, if you like you can take over Receipts and Disbursements."

Rappoport stared. "Commissioner of Receipts and Disbursements?"

"I can go higher if you want. Fancier. Board of Water Supply's a dandy. Nice remuneration, practically no show."

"Ruth, Ruth, what is this?"

Justice, justice shalt thou pursue!

It is Mayor Puttermesser's first political deal.

"Stay a night in Xanthippe's bed and any job you want is yours. The orchard's dropping into your lap, Morris, I'm serious. Plums."

"A spot in your Administration actually?"

"Why not? Choose."

"Receipts and Disbursements," Rappoport instantly replies.

Puttermesser says sourly, "You're at least as qualified as Turtelman."

"What about my wife?"

"Keep her in Toronto."

Standing in solitude in the night fragrance behind Gracie Mansion, Puttermesser catches river-gleams: the Circle Line yacht with its chandelier decks; a neon sign pulsing; the distant caps of little waves glinting in moonwake, in neonwake. White bread baking on the night shift casts its faintly animal aroma on the waters: rich fumes more savory than any blossom. It is so dark in the back garden that Puttermesser imagines she can almost descry Orion's belt buckle. One big moving star twins as it sails: the headlights of an airliner nosing out toward Europe. Plane after plane rises, as if out of the black river. Puttermesser counts them, each with its sharp beams like rays scattered from the brow of Moses, arching upward into the fathomless universe. She counts planes; she counts neon blinks; she counts the silhouettes of creeping scows; she counts all the mayors who have preceded her in the City of New York. Thomas Willett, Thomas Delavall . . .

William Dervall, Nicholas De Meyer, Stephanus Van Cort-
landt . . . Francis Rombouts . . . Isaac de Reimer, Thomas
Noell, Philip French, William Peartree, Ebenezer Wilson . . .
DeWitt Clinton . . . Gideon Lee . . . Smith Ely . . . Jimmy
Walker . . . John P. O'Brien, Fiorello H. LaGuardia . . .
Robert F. Wagner, John V. Lindsay, Abraham D. Beame,
Edward I. Koch! She counts and waits. She is waiting for the
golem to be lured homeward, to be ensnared, to lumber
groaning with desire into her fourposter bed.

In the golem's fourposter, Commissioner Morris Rappoport, newly appointed chief of the Department of Receipts
and Disbursements, lies in sheets saturated with a certain
known pungency. He has been here before. He recoils from
the familiar scented pillows.

Indoors and out, odors of what has been and what is about
to be: the cook's worn eggplant au gratin, river smells, the
garden beating its tiny wings of so many fresh hedge-leaves,
airplane exhaust spiraling downward, the fine keen breath of
the bread ovens, the golem's perfumed pillows—all these
drifting smokes and combinations stir and turn and braid
themselves into a rope of awesome incense, drawing Xanthippe to her bed. Incense? Fetor and charged decay! The
acrid signal of dissolution! Intimations of the tellurian elements! Xanthippe, from wherever she has hurtled to in the
savage City (savage once again), is pulled nearer and nearer
the Mansion, where the portraits of dead mayors hang. Scepter and status, all the enchantments of influence and command, lead her to her undoing: in her bed lies the extremely
important official whose job it is to call the tune that makes
the City's money dance. She will burst on him her giant love.
On the newly appointed Commissioner of Receipts and Disbursements the golem will spend her terrible ardor. Then she
will fall back to rest, among the awful perfumes of her cleft
bed.

Whereupon Mayor Puttermesser, her term of office

blighted, her comely *PLAN* betrayed, will dismantle the golem, according to the rite.

XI. THE GOLEM UNDONE, AND THE BABBLING OF RAPPOPORT

The City was ungovernable; the City was out of control; it was no different now for Mayor Puttermesser than it had ever been for any mayor. In confusion and hypocrisy, Puttermesser finished out what was left of her sovereign days.

One thing was different: a certain tumulus of earth introduced by the Parks Commissioner in the mournful latter half of Mayor Puttermesser's Administration.

Across the street from City Hall lies a little park, crisscrossed by paths and patches of lawn fenced off by black iron staves. There are benches set down here and there with a scattered generosity. There is even an upward-flying fountain. Perhaps because the little park is in the shadow of City Hall and, so to speak, under its surveillance, the benches have not been seriously vandalized, and the lawns not much trampled on. Best of all, and most alluring, are the flower beds, vivid rectangles of red geraniums disposed, it must be admitted, in the design of a miniature graveyard. Civil servants peering down from high windows of the elephant-gray Municipal Building can see the crimson slash that with wild brilliance cuts across the concrete bitterness below. Some distance behind the flower beds rise those great Stonehenge slabs of the Twin Towers; eastward, the standing zither that is Brooklyn Bridge.

From the Mayor's office inside City Hall the park is not visible, and for Puttermesser this is just as well. It would not have done for her to be in sight of Xanthippe's bright barrow while engaged in City business. Under the roots of the flower

beds lay fresh earth, newly put down and lightly tamped.
Mayor Puttermesser herself, in the middle of the night, had
telephoned the Parks Commissioner (luckily just back from
Paris.) and ordered the ground to be opened and a crudely
formed and crumbling mound of special soil to be arranged in
the cavity, as in an envelope of earth. The Parks Commissioner, urgently summoned, thought it odd, when he arrived
at Gracie Mansion with his sleepy diggers, that the Mayor
should be pacing in the back garden behind the Mansion
under a veined half-moon; and odder yet that she should be
accompanied by a babbling man with a sliding tongue, who
identified himself as the newly appointed Commissioner of
Receipts and Disbursements, Morris Rappoport.

"Did you bring spades? And a pickup truck?" the Mayor
whispered.

"All of that, yes."

"Well, the spades won't do. At least not yet. You don't
shovel up a floor. You can use the spades afterward, in the
park. There's some dried mud spread out on a bedroom floor
in the Mansion. I want it moved. With very great delicacy.
Can you make your men understand that?"

"Dried mud?"

"I grant you it's in pieces. It's already falling apart. But it's
got a certain design. Be delicate."

What the Parks Commissioner saw was a very large and
shapeless, or mainly shapeless, mound of soil, insanely
wrapped (so the Parks Commissioner privately judged) in a
kind of velvet shroud. The Parks Commissioner had been on
an official exchange program in France, and had landed at
Kennedy Airport less than two hours before the Mayor telephoned. The exchange program meant that he would study
the enchanting parks of Paris, while his Parisian counterpart
was to consider the gloomier parks of New York. The Parks
Commissioner, of course, was Puttermesser's own appointee,
a botanist and city planner, an expert on the hardiness of

certain shade trees, a specialist in filigreed gazebos, a lover of the urban nighttime. All the same, he was perplexed by the Mayor's caprice. The mound of dirt on the bedroom floor did not suggest to him his own good fortune and near escape. In fact, though neither would ever learn this, the Parks Commissioner and his Parisian counterpart were both under a felicitous star—the Parisian because his wife's appendectomy had kept him unexpectedly and rather too lengthily in Paris so that he never arrived in New York at all (he was an anxious man), and the Parks Commissioner because he had not been at home in his lower Fifth Avenue bed when the golem came to call. Instead, he had been out inspecting the Bois de Boulogne—consequently, the Parks Commissioner was in fine mental health, and was shocked to observe that the newly appointed Commissioner of Receipts and Disbursements was not.

Rappoport babbled. He followed after Puttermesser like a dog. He had performed exactly as she had instructed, it seemed, but then her instructions became contradictory. First he was to circle. Then he was not to circle. Rather, he was to scrape with his penknife. There he was, all at once a satrap with a title; the title was as palpable as a mantle, and as sumptuous; overhead drooped the fourposter's white velvet canopy with its voluptuous folds and snowy crevices—how thickly warm his title, how powerful his office! Alone, enclosed in the authority of his rank, Rappoport awaited the visitation of the golem. Without a stitch, not a shred of sari remaining, her burnished gaze on fire with thirst for his grandeur, she burst in, redolent of beaches, noisy with a fiery hiss; Rappoport tore the white velvet from the tester and threw it over burning Xanthippe.

Rappoport babbled. He told all the rest: how they had contended; how he had endured her size and force and the horror of her immodesty and the awful sea of her sweat and the sirocco of her summer breath; and how he—or was it she?

—had chanted out the hundred proud duties of his new juris-diction: the protocol and potency of the City's money, where it is engendered, where it is headed, where it lands: it could be said that she was teaching him his job. And then the Mayor, speaking through the door, explaining the depth of tranquility after potency that is deeper than any sleep or drug or anes-thesia, directing him to remove Xanthippe in all her dead-weight mass from the fourposter down to the bare floor, and to wind her in the canopy.

Rappoport babbled: how he had lifted Xanthippe in her trance, the torpor that succeeds ravishment, down to the bare floor; how he had wound her in white velvet; how pale Putter-messer, her reading lenses glimmering into an old green book, directed him with sharpened voice to crowd his mind with impurity—with everything earthly, soiled, spoiled, wormy; finally how Puttermesser directed him to trail her as she weaved round Xanthippe on the floor, as if circling her own shadow.

Round and round Puttermesser went. In the instant of giv-ing the golem life, the just, the comely, the cleanly, the Edenic, had, all unwittingly, consummated Puttermesser's aspiring reflections—even the radiant *PLAN* itself! Now all must be consciously reversed. She must think of violent-eyed loiterers who lurk in elevators with springblades at the ready, of spray cans gashing red marks of civilization-hate, of civic monuments with their heads knocked off, of City filth, of mugging, robbery, arson, assault, even murder. Murder! If, for life, she had dreamed Paradise, now she must feel the burning lance of hell. If, for life, she had walked seven times clockwise round a hillock of clay, now she must walk seven times counterclockwise round captive Xanthippe. If, for life, she had pronounced the Name, now she must on no account speak or imagine it or lend it any draught or flame of breath; she must erase the Name utterly.

And what of Rappoport, Rappoport the golem's lure and snare, Rappoport who had played himself out in the capture of Xanthippe? He too must walk counterclockwise, behind Puttermesser, just as the Great Rabbi Judah Loew had walked counterclockwise with his disciples when the time came for the golem of Prague to be undone. The golem of Prague, city-savior, had also run amok!—terrorizing the very citizens it had been created to succor. And all the rites the Great Rabbi Judah Loew had pondered in the making of the golem, he ultimately dissolved in the unmaking of it. All the permutations and combinations of the alphabet he had recited with profound and holy concentration in the golem's creation, he afterward declaimed backward, for the sake of the golem's discomposition. Instead of meditating on the building up, he meditated on the breaking down. Whatever he had early spiraled, he late unraveled: he smashed the magnetic links that formed the chain of being between the atoms.

Puttermesser, circling round the torpid Xanthippe in her shroud of white velvet, could not help glancing down into the golem's face. It was a child's face still. Ah, Leah, Leah! Xanthippe's lids flickered. Xanthippe's lips stirred. She looked with her terrible eyes—how they pulsed—up at Puttermesser.

"My mother."

A voice!

"O my mother," Xanthippe said, still looking upward at Puttermesser, "why are you walking around me like that?"

She spoke! Her voice ascended!—a child's voice, pitched like the pure cry of a bird.

Puttermesser did not halt. "Keep moving," she told Rappoport.

"O my mother," Xanthippe said in her bird-quick voice, "why are you walking around me like that?"

Beginning the fifth circle, Rappoport gasping behind her, Puttermesser said, "You created and you destroyed."

"No," the golem cried—the power of speech released!—"it was you who created me, it is you who will destroy me! Life! Love! Mercy! Love! Life!"

The fifth circle was completed; still the golem went on bleating in her little bird's cry. "Life! Life! More!"

"More," Puttermesser said bitterly, beginning the sixth circle. "More. You wanted more and more. It's more that brought us here. More!"

"You wanted Paradise!"

"Too much Paradise is greed. Eden disintegrates from too much Eden. Eden sinks from a surfeit of itself."

"O my mother! I made you Mayor!"

Completing the sixth circle, Puttermesser said, "You pulled the City down."

"O my mother! Do not cool my heat!"

Beginning the seventh circle, Puttermesser said, "This is the last. Now go home."

"O my mother! Do not send me to the elements!"

The seventh circle was completed; the golem's small voice piped on. Xanthippe lay stretched at Puttermesser's feet like Puttermesser's own shadow.

"Trouble," Puttermesser muttered. "Somehow this isn't working, Morris. Maybe because you're not a priest or a Levite."

Rappoport swallowed a tremulous breath. "If she gets to stand, if she decides to haul herself up—"

"Morris," Puttermesser said, "do you have a pocket knife?"

Rappoport took one out.

"O my mother, mother of my life!" the golem bleated. "Only think how for your sake I undid Turtelman, Marmel, Mavett!"

Huge sly Xanthippe, gargantuan wily Xanthippe, grown up out of the little seed of a dream of Leah!

Rappoport, obeying Puttermesser, blew aside the golem's

bangs and with his small blade erased from Xanthippe's forehead what appeared to be no more than an old scar—the first on the right of three such scars—queerly in the shape of a sort of letter K.

Instantly the golem shut her lips and eyes.

The *aleph* was gone.

"Dead," Rappoport said.

"Returned," Puttermesser said. "Carry her up to the attic."

"The attic? *Here?* In Gracie Mansion? Ruth, think!"

"The Great Rabbi Judah Loew undid the golem of Prague in the attic of the Altneuschul. A venerable public structure, Morris, no less estimable than Gracie Mansion."

Rappoport laughed out loud. Then he let his tongue slide out, back and forth, from right to left, along the corners of his mouth.

"Bend down, Morris."

Rappoport bent down.

"Pick up her left hand. By the wrist, that's the way."

Between Rappoport's forefinger and thumb the golem's left hand broke into four clods.

"No, it won't do. This wasn't well planned, Morris, I admit it. If we try to get her up the attic stairs—well, you can see what's happening. Never mind, I'll call the Parks Commissioner. Maybe City Hall Park—"

Then began the babbling of Rappoport.

XII. UNDER THE FLOWER BEDS

Garbage trucks are back on the streets. Their ferocious grinders gnash the City's spew. Traffic fumes, half a hundred cars immobile in a single intersection, demoralization in the ladies' lavatories of the Municipal Building, computers down,

Albany at war with City Hall, a drop in fifth-grade reading scores—the City is choking. It cannot be governed. It cannot be controlled. There is a rumor up from Florida that ex-Mayor Malachy ("Matt") Mavett is scheming to recapture City Hall. As for current patronage, there is the egregious case of the newly appointed Commissioner of Receipts and Disbursements, said to be the Mayor's old lover; he resigns for health reasons even before taking office. His wife fetches him home to Toronto. Mayor Puttermesser undergoes periodontal surgery. When it is over, the roots of her teeth are exposed. Inside the secret hollow of her head, just below the eye sockets, on the lingual side, she is unendingly conscious of her own skeleton.

The *Soho News* is the only journal to note the Mayor's order, in the middle of a summer night, for an extra load of dirt to be shoveled under the red geraniums of City Hall Park. Parks Department diggers have planted a small wooden marker among the flower beds: DO NOT TOUCH OR PICK. With wanton contempt for civic decorum, passersby often flout the modest sign. Yet whoever touches or picks those stems of blood-colored blossoms soon sickens with flu virus, or sore throat, or stuffed nose accompanied by nausea—or, sometimes, a particularly vicious attack of bursitis.

And all the while Puttermesser calls in her heart: O lost New York! And she calls: O lost Xanthippe!

Obelisk

The following is a list of Obelisk titles now available, each chosen as an example of excellent prose:

Donald Barthelme, *Sixty Stories*

Noël Coward, *Pomp and Circumstance*

Jane Howard, *A Different Woman*

Molly Keane, *Good Behaviour*

Peter Matthiessen, *The Tree Where Man Was Born*

Joyce Carol Oates, *A Sentimental Education*

Cynthia Ozick, *Levitation*
The Pagan Rabbi and Other Stories

Oliver Sacks, *Awakenings*

Raymond Sokolov, *Fading Feast*
Native Intelligence

W. M. Spackman, *A Presence with Secrets*

Jean Stafford, *The Mountain Lion*

Calvin Tomkins, *Living Well Is the Best Revenge*